"Put Your Hands Under My Coat. Got To Warm Up."

He obeyed without question, pressing himself close to the warmth of her body and pushing his hands beneath her coat, against her back.

She tugged his blanket around them both. "If you...try anything f-funny," she added belatedly, her voice muffled by the blankets, "I'll...k-kill you."

It was a moment before he replied, between irregular breaths, "If I tried anything...funny, the effort would probably kill me."

It was a long time before Pam could think about anything except how miserable she was. The racking shivers, the stiffness in her limbs, took precedence over whatever awkwardness she might otherwise have felt at finding herself wrapped in an intimate embrace with a stranger whose name she didn't even know.

"How do you feel?" she felt compelled to ask after a time.

His face was burrowed beneath the blankets, and he didn't look up to reply. "I hope you won't take this personally—" his arms tightened around her and he shivered again "—but...I've had better dates."

Dear Reader:

So many of you asked for him, and now you've got him: Shiloh Butler, Mr. November. *Shiloh's Promise* by BJ James, is the long-awaited sequel to *Twice in a Lifetime*. Not only do many of your favorite characters reappear, but the enigmatic and compelling Shiloh now has his very own story—and his own woman!

And coming in December... *Wilderness Child* by Ann Major. This tie-in to her *Children of Destiny* series winds up 1989 in a very exciting way....

I've been telling you so much about the *Man of the Month* program that I want to mention some other exciting plans we have in store for you. Celeste Hamilton will be starting a trilogy in December with *The Diamond's Sparkle*. And the next few months will be bringing you Desires from such favorites as Katherine Granger, Linda Lael Miller and Dixie Browning....

So go wild with Desire—you'll be glad you did!

All the best,

Lucia Macro
Senior Editor

DONNA
CARLISLE

INTERLUDE

SILHOUETTE *Desire*

Published by Silhouette Books New York

America's Publisher of Contemporary Romance

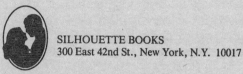

SILHOUETTE BOOKS
300 East 42nd St., New York, N.Y. 10017

ISBN: 0-373-05530-7

First Silhouette Books printing November 1989

Printed in the U.S.A.

Books by Donna Carlisle

Silhouette Desire

Under Cover #417
A Man Around the House #476
Interlude #530

DONNA CARLISLE

lives in Atlanta, Georgia, with her teenage daughter. Weekends and summers are spent in her rustic north Georgia cabin, where she enjoys hiking, painting and planning her next novel.

Donna has also written under the pseudonyms Rebecca Flanders and Leigh Bristol.

One

The last thing Alan saw was a fox dashing across the road.

The snow had been whipping across Alan's windshield faster than the wiper blades could clear it; had he been paying attention he would have noticed that the storm had increased its fury some miles back and that the narrow mountain road had long since ceased to be negotiable by prudent drivers. But Alan hadn't been paying attention. His mind had been on other things when a flash of reddish-brown fur darted across his field of vision and he'd reacted instinctively. He'd hit the brakes, and the car had fishtailed and spun crazily, and he'd had time to think two things. The first was, *What is that poor animal doing out on a day like this?* And the next, *It's true. Your life really does flash before your eyes.* . . .

In an instant he relived it all: the fire-engine-shaped cake at his third birthday party, finding a sand dollar at the beach when he was five, kissing Mary Kelly behind the concession stand at the football game, a thousand details, up to and including the fury and contempt in his father's eyes yesterday just before Alan had stormed out the door. The car plowed into a snowbank; Alan's seat belt locked across his chest with a force that felt sufficient to have cracked some ribs, and he was flung back against the seat. But he didn't mind the pain; it was better than reliving the past. Besides, it meant he was alive, and if he had had any doubts before, Alan had discovered within the last few seconds that alive was a very good thing to be.

He sat there stunned, breathing hard, and waited for his head to clear. After a time he became aware of the sound of snow pelting the roof and the slow, irregular click of the Porsche's cooling engine. In combination, those were two very lonely and eerie sounds.

Gingerly he unfastened his seat belt and began to check for damage. He rubbed the back of his neck, which didn't hurt too badly, and flexed his arms and legs as much as the seat would allow. The muscles across his shoulders were sore, but he was relieved to discover his ribs didn't appear to be broken. All in all, he figured he'd come off pretty well.

He turned the key halfheartedly and was rewarded with an unsatisfactory click. Scowling, he folded his arms across his chest, then winced at the discomfort that caused and braced his arms against the steering wheel again. "As somebody somewhere is undoubtedly saying at this moment," he muttered, "it serves you right."

A blast of wind rocked the car on its axis, flinging a curtain of snow across the windows, and Alan looked around worriedly. When had the weather turned so foul, and how had he failed to notice? God, where had his mind been? But he knew the answer to that, and berating himself for his stupidity wasn't going to improve his situation any. With a half-swallowed curse, he opened the door and got out.

His boots sank ankle-deep into the snow just before an explosion of arctic wind knocked him back against the car. Icy needles stung his cheeks and whipped across his neck. Gasping, he stumbled back inside and pulled the door closed behind him.

Forgetting the ache in his shoulders, he rubbed his arms furiously against the shivers and murmured choppily, "This could be more serious than you thought."

Quickly, he took stock of the situation and it didn't look good. He had no idea where he was, and though he racked his brain he couldn't remember seeing a service station or a telephone since he had turned off the main highway an indeterminate number of miles back. Not that he was inclined to walk in this weather, anyway—aside from an occasional ski trip during which he made a point to spend more time in the lodge than on the slopes, his experience with snow was limited, and he liked it that way.

He tightened his fists briefly on the steering wheel and said, "Damn." Lost in a snowstorm on a deserted mountain highway, his car disabled and his emergency supplies nil—things couldn't get much worse.

But no. Defeatism wasn't in his nature and he refused to give in to despair. Any man who could negotiate the hazards of the Amazon and cross a desert on camel-back could certainly handle this. "All right," he said aloud after a moment. "Serious, but not critical."

Of course, neither the Amazon nor the African desert was known for its blizzards, and Alan hadn't gone into either of them alone and unprepared. But it was against all logic that he, Alan Bartholomew Donovan, should meet his end in a snowbank in one of the most populated countries in the world. There was always the Highway Patrol, after all. "It might just take a little time," he assured himself. "Someone will come along."

The sound of his own voice cheered him somewhat, and he turned to retrieve his duffel bag from the backseat. The warmest thing he could find was an alpaca sweater, which he quickly slipped over his head. He lowered the window a crack for ventilation, turned the ignition key to Auxiliary, and pushed the heater controls all the way forward. Then he huddled down in the seat, spreading his hands before the warm blast of air from the vents, and settled down to wait.

* * *

I don't love you anymore. Pam turned the words over and over in her head, curiously and cautiously, studying them with the thorough, absorbed detachment of one who was learning a new language. She kept waiting for the pain, the outrage, the shock and betrayal, but they never came. In fact, what she felt was strangely akin to relief—like kicking off a pair of shoes that you'd discovered were too tight at the end of the day.

It had all been very calm and very civilized, just as everything was with Peter. She had driven to Denver to welcome her fiancé home after a two-year absence, and right there in the airport terminal he had told her. *He might have at least written me a letter,* she thought irritably as she hunched over the steering wheel and squinted through the driving snow, *instead of bringing me out in the worst storm of the year, sixty miles to Denver and then back again....*

The radio reported that the weather was getting worse and higher elevations were gearing up for a full-force blizzard. Wolf Creek Pass had already been closed, which was why Pam had taken the Old Canyon Road. It was not, perhaps, the best choice, because it was rarely traveled in the winter and snowplows hardly ever made it out this far. But it cut ten miles off her trip, and Pam had had some vague notion of outrunning the storm. Obviously, she hadn't succeeded.

There was another woman, of course. At least Peter had been honest enough to admit that. She was a research psychologist, and although Peter had not described her to Pam she could picture her in her mind: tall, elegant, sophisticated. The perfect hostess, the perfect companion, and all in all a far better match for Peter than Pam had been.

Her back tires skidded a little on the turn and she quickly brought her attention back to her driving. Pamela Mercer was a mountain girl by birth, she knew every twist and curve in this road, wet or dry, and her four-wheel drive was properly equipped with snow chains. She was a cautious driver and there was no reason she shouldn't make it home safely—if she kept her mind on the road and off the Denver airport, where even now a jet was bearing Peter off to New York City and the arms of his new love.

I guess I'd better tell Mom to cancel the engagement party, she thought dolefully, and that was when she saw the red gleam of an automobile's taillights across her path.

She was startled and lost a second's reaction time as she tried to make out the position of the car through the snow. When she swerved, the steering wheel spun wildly through her fingers, and for an endless moment she saw nothing but whirling snow and crazily tilting sky.

The car came to a jolting, slamming stop, and Pam watched in dull amazement as dust drifted down in feathery clouds from the overhead upholstery. She let out a shuddering moan, and forcefully unwound her fingers from the steering wheel. She was all right. She was alive.

The car was canted at a forty-five degree angle, which made it difficult for Pam to unfasten her seat belt and push open the door—especially since she was shaking so badly she could hardly make her fingers work. When she stepped outside her feet slid out from under her and she tumbled four feet down a snowbank.

She came to rest on her hands and knees, sputtering and shaking the snow out of her mouth. When she looked up a man was coming toward her. With the snow coming down in sheets and being kicked up in clouds by the wind, she could see little of him besides the fact that he was tall and slim, and had the most startling helmet of silver-blond hair she had ever seen—at least she thought the color was silver. Considering the fact that he was wearing nothing but lightweight khaki trousers and an alpaca sweater in temperatures that were fast approaching zero, the color of his hair might have been due to no more than a frosting of ice.

"Are you all right?" he shouted.

He trudged slowly through the snow, and by the time he reached her Pam had managed to regain her feet. Up close, she could tell that he was young, her age or a little older. And his hair *was* silver, the pure platinum blond of a very young child, and even in the dull light of the overcast day, tossed and parted viciously by the brutal wind, it gleamed with a life of its own. She had never seen hair like that before, not in real life.

"Are you hurt?" he repeated, raising his voice to be heard above the wind.

Pam looked around until she caught the gleam of headlights behind her. Her car had actually come to rest in front of the car that had caused the accident, and her relief at not having hit him was almost immediately replaced by indignation. "Is that your car?" she demanded.

"Well, I didn't exactly walk here." Shivering and hugging his arms in the snow, he seemed a little indignant himself.

"Why didn't you turn on your emergency lights? Are you crazy, leaving your car blocking the road like that? Don't you realize I almost hit you? We both could have been killed!"

Without giving him a chance to reply she whirled back to her own car. "Look at my car!"

He pushed his hair back from his face with one hand, tucking the other under his armpit to warm it. "Looks almost as bad as mine!" he shouted back, and Pam felt a small stab of remorse. He had not, after all, purposefully driven his car into a snowbank just to inconvenience her.

The wind whipped through her like a knife, and she flipped the hood of her quilted parka over her head, fumbling in her pockets for her gloves as she made her way around the car. It was worse than she had expected. The two front wheels were solidly lodged in a bank, the other two dangled over a ditch. There was no way that vehicle could be gotten onto the road under its own power.

"Can you get your car started?" she shouted to the man behind her.

He stamped his feet and slapped his hands against his arms as the wind gusted. "What?"

She gestured. "Maybe we can get your car out and use it to push mine—"

He shook his head. "Engine won't start!"

The wind whipped around her legs beneath her coat and she shivered, glancing at the sky. "We've got to do something! This isn't letting up!"

"Can we talk about it inside?"

"What?"

He gestured toward his car and then, head ducked against the wind, started toward it at a half run. Pam followed him because she couldn't get back into her car without climbing up a snowbank.

She pulled the door closed and sank back into the luxurious interior of the Porsche, gasping from the exercise. He was huddled behind the steering wheel, shivering so hard she could hear his teeth chatter. He was a fool for going out without his coat.

It was warm inside the car, and it took Pam a minute to realize why. When she did she gasped, and quickly leaned forward to push the heater controls off. "Are you trying to kill yourself?"

"The window is open," he protested, and reached for the controls.

"Your exhaust pipe is buried in the snow! All those fumes are coming right back into the car. Can't you smell them?"

He hesitated, then let his hand drop from the controls. "I guess I didn't notice."

She stared at him incredulously. "Another half hour and you would have been dead from carbon-monoxide poisoning."

He sank back against the seat dejectedly. "This doesn't appear to be my day." And then he offered her a vague and rather forced grin. "Good thing you came along, huh?"

Pam wiped the melting snow off her face with the back of a gloved hand. "Right. Just in time to wreck my car, save your life, and leave us both stranded in the middle of a blizzard. I have a knack for things like that."

He shrugged. "Fate works in mysterious ways."

His lack of concern over the seriousness of their situation baffled Pam, but she had other things to worry about and didn't spare him much of her attention. Both of their cars were disabled, and in these temperatures, even sheltered from the wind, they couldn't last more than a few hours. Even more frightening was the thought of the snow drifting up and covering the car, trapping them in an icy tomb. Every winter the news was spotted with reports of the tragic fates of stranded travelers; Pamela had no intention of becoming another one of those statistics.

There was no car phone on the dashboard, nor a CB mike. Pam's own CB had gone on the blink a month ago and she cursed herself for not having it fixed sooner. But there were so many more important things to do with her paycheck—clothes to buy, a new pair of boots, a welcome-home present for Peter...

Sternly she jerked her thoughts back to the immediate crisis, and directed her eyes out the window, scanning the countryside to get her bearings. Relief came over her in a wave.

"I know where we are." She wiped the fog from the window and pointed. "If we cut through the woods, McMurty's cabin is just over that hill. It's closed up now, but there might be a telephone."

He leaned over to peer through the window. "I don't see anything."

"Well, I didn't say it would be easy. But it's not all that far—closer than hiking back to the highway, anyway. And it won't be dark for a while. We won't get lost."

He frowned. Out of the wind and snow, Pam was able to see him for the first time. His face was narrow and sharp-boned, with a hawkish nose and battle-ship-gray eyes. His skin, though still ruddy and chapped from the cold, was smooth and unlined, with just the faintest hint of a pale gold tan—not an honest ski tan, or an outdoor workman's tan, but the kind of cosmetic tan that comes from a salon. He did have an interesting mouth though, his lips distinctively formed and so perfectly etched they might have been designed by an artist's brush. His eyebrows, in contrast to the startling platinum hair, were dark, and the effect was dramatic. Some people might even consider him attractive. Pam might have if the circumstances had been different.

He said cautiously, "What do you mean, 'We'?"

She expelled a breath of exasperation. "You don't mean you just want to sit here?"

"Why not?" He seemed completely unconcerned. "Somebody will be along."

She stared at him. "Haven't you been listening to the radio?"

He tapped the console. "Tape deck."

"Well for your information, we're in the middle of a blizzard. Mountain blizzards are serious business. Roads are closed during blizzards. People don't leave their houses during blizzards. And nobody is going to come by here. Even if they did, they would probably be worse off than we are. We can't just sit here and wait. We'll freeze."

The frown hovered around his brow again as he seemed to consider this. Then his expression lightened as he gave a dismissive shrug. "It can't be that bad. Somebody will come. Somebody always comes." And he grinned. "*You* came."

Pam gave an impatient shake of her head and zipped up her coat. "Stay here if you want," she said, firmly tying the drawstring of her hood. "I'm going to try to find a telephone. I'll send somebody back for you if I can."

She opened the door and forged out into the snow, drawing her scarf up over her mouth and lower face. Pam had taken perhaps five steps into the driving wind when she heard a shout behind her. She wasn't particularly surprised when she looked back and saw the silver-haired young Porsche driver following her, his long-legged stride kicking up puffs of snow as he hurried to catch up.

"It wouldn't be very gallant of me to let you go off alone, would it?" he explained cheerfully as he drew up beside her. He was carrying a tan leather duffel over his shoulder, and was still wearing nothing but the light sweater over his clothes.

"Where is your coat?" she demanded. The wind threatened to whip her words away even though she shouted.

He shrugged, pushing a handful of hair out of his eyes, which the wind immediately tossed back again. "Don't have one."

"Are you crazy?"

"It wasn't snowing in California!"

She threw up a hand. "Wait here!"

She struggled back to her car and returned a few moments later with a flashlight and two blankets, which she kept in the trunk for emergencies. "Wrap these around you," she instructed. Her voice was beginning to crack from the effort to make herself heard above the wind. "And try to keep your hands in your pockets!"

He grinned and tossed the blankets nonchalantly over one shoulder. Pam tucked the flashlight into the pocket of her parka and led the way.

Five minutes later the blankets were wrapped around both shoulders and he struggled to keep the ends together while trying to protect his hands from the bitter cold. Pamela parted with her wool scarf, which he gratefully and wordlessly tied over his head. It was an uphill climb, fraught with snow-covered undergrowth and heavy, low-hanging limbs, and he was falling far behind. At first Pam didn't wait for him— the cold was agonizing when she stood still—but after a while her conscience overcame the discomfort.

She half trudged, half slid down the hill a dozen or so yards back to him, muttering epithets under her breath descriptive of the kind of fool who would brave a Rocky Mountain winter in a pair of cotton pants and a pullover sweater. "California, naturally," she grunted, just before she reached him. "Where else?"

She grabbed his arm and raised her voice. "Are you okay?"

"No, I'm not okay!" he shouted back at her. "Do I look okay?"

His face was a raw, chapped red, and rimed with flakes of snow. And the ends of his hair were stiff where sweat and melted snow had frozen. Pam realized with an uncomfortable stab of alarm that frostbite was a very definite possibility.

With the scarf tied around his ears and his shoulders hunched beneath the blankets there was, however, an element of the absurd, and she would have laughed if the situation hadn't been so dire. "You look," she informed him, "like something out of *Pilgrim's Progress*—or like somebody just crazy enough to be born in California!"

"*I'm* crazy? Whose idea was it to cross the Continental Divide in the middle of a blizzard?"

"Come on!" She tugged at his arm and determinedly set forth again.

As they moved deeper into the woods there was some shelter from the wind, but the snow was just as heavy, and their difficulties were compounded by chunks that fell from the branches and drifts that were formed as they moved. Pam's feet were like blocks of ice, her lungs ached and her cheeks were numb. Her companion kept up, although with obvious effort. His breathing was just as labored as her own, and his feet, without the advantage of the woolen socks Pam wore, moved much more slowly.

"Besides," he said between heavy breaths some time later, "I wasn't born in California. I was born in Istanbul."

She spared him a brief, suspicious glance, but decided he was just making conversation to keep his mind off the cold—which wasn't a bad idea. If Pam could have spared the breath, she would have reciprocated, but settled for mental reassurance instead.

Though back in the car she could have traced the route to McMurty's cabin blindfolded, the longer they struggled against the cold and the snow the less sure she became of her direction. She hadn't really been paying much attention to where she was before the accident, and in the snow the landmarks might look different...suppose they were in actuality miles away from where she thought?

No, she assured herself. That was impossible. She had spent half her life patrolling these roads with her father, in sun, rain and snow. She couldn't make a mistake like that. But she had never actually climbed through the woods from the road to the cabin; the more direct approach was via an old logging road that ran off the main highway about five miles to the east. She knew where the cabin was supposed to be, and she knew it could, theoretically, be reached through these woods. But suppose she was wrong? Suppose she was leading them in circles? Suppose they came upon a deadfall or an unfordable stream or some other unforeseen impediment and had to turn back?

The smallest stirrings of panic began in her. Though the exercise was causing her to sweat beneath her heavy clothes she could tell the temperature was dropping rapidly and whenever they passed through a clearing and were exposed to the brunt of the wind the cold was agonizing. And if she was suffering, as fully prepared for the weather as she was, how long could her companion be expected to hold out? People *died* in conditions like these.

It can't be much farther, she insisted to herself, firmly pushing the morbid doubts away. No, she wasn't lost, and she wasn't wrong about the cabin and once they got there they were going to be fine. . . .

"Cold, isn't it?" the young man beside her offered with an attempt at nonchalance that was laudable— and would have been effective, if his teeth had not been chattering so badly that the words were almost indistinguishable.

"I've been colder," Pam replied, but her own voice was stiff with trying to hold back shivers, and punctuated with gasps for breath. "I just can't remember when, right now."

"Is it much farther?"

"No," she lied, and grabbed his arm again, as much for support to her own aching legs as to urge him toward the top of the hill.

How strange it was. When she had started out, the plan had seemed so simple: climb through the woods and over the hill to McMurty's cabin, where there would be shelter, warmth, and possibly a telephone. No big deal; in fact she had congratulated herself on thinking of it.

But it was no longer a simple thing; no longer easy or clear-cut. It was, in fact, the biggest challenge Pam had ever faced in her life. When they moved out into the open the wind was so punishing it was all she could do to put one foot in front of the other in a straight line. When the wind hissed down the opening of her hood or cut across her jeaned legs the pain actually brought tears to her eyes—which she could not shed for fear they would freeze on her cheeks.

Time blurred into a meaningless collage of trudging footsteps and harsh breathing. Snow slashed against her face and she couldn't see. She couldn't feel her feet anymore and the effort required to pick them up and put them down again made her feel as if she was lifting lead weights. Her throat and lungs burned, and she could hear little sobbing sounds that she vaguely realized were coming from her. She began to have macabre thoughts about the Donner party, who had become lost in the mountains in the eighteen hundreds and had survived the winter by eating the bodies of their dead. Sometimes it seemed she had been walking forever, and sometimes it seemed like only a few minutes. But it didn't matter, because regardless of how long she walked she never seemed to get anywhere.

Sometimes she forgot about the man walking beside her entirely, sometimes it seemed as though he was the only thing that was keeping her going. When she glanced at him and saw how drawn and grim his face was, how stiff his muscles were as he huddled beneath the meager protection of the blankets, she thought

helplessly, *I'm sorry. I'm sorry I got you into this....*
But she didn't have the strength to tell him so.

When she saw the dim, snow-covered shape mate-
rialize in the distance Pam was too exhausted, too
dulled by cold and pain, to even feel relief. She wordlessly continued toward it.

The snow was already high enough to cover the
bottom step that lead to the small covered porch, and
Pam tripped over it and went sprawling. She was
hardly even aware of the strong arm pulling her to her
feet again. She half crawled, half stumbled onto the
porch.

Her companion leaned heavily against the wall as
Pam pulled herself to her full height, then on tiptoe,
and stretched her gloved hand over the doorjamb. Her
fingers closed on the key, and after three fumbling
tries, she got it into the lock. She pushed open the
door and the two of them stumbled inside.

Two

Lionel McMurty was vice president in charge of production of one of the most profitable manufacturing firms in Raintree County, and the cabin was only one of three residences he owned in Colorado. He had built the cabin for, in his own words, "autumn hunting, spring trout fishing and summertime rocking on the porch." It was therefore just rustic enough to serve as a pleasant refuge from a high-pressure world, but not so provincial as to overlook modern conveniences such as plumbing and electricity.

It was well insulated and snug, constructed of sturdy logs on the outside and solid oak planking on the inside. One large room with exposed beams contained the kitchen, sleeping area and a casual seating group which, in the summertime, looked out over a beautiful wooded hillside and the trout stream below. Now, however, the picture windows were closed off with bolted storm shutters, the furniture was draped in dust covers, and it was dark and musty smelling inside. And cold. It was still very, very cold.

It took a while for Pam's head to clear, and for her eyes to adjust to the dimness. The first thing she saw was the Franklin stove situated in the middle of a fieldstone hearth on the opposite wall. All she could think about was how *cold* she was. Her teeth were chattering convulsively and she could barely control the racking shivers long enough to make her legs cross the floor to the stove.

There was a neat stack of firewood next to it and when she wrenched the door open she found that, typical of mountain hospitality and preparedness, a fire had already been laid, awaiting the strike of a match. *God bless you, Mr. McMurty,* she thought, and tugged her glove off with her teeth. There was a container of fireplace matches on the hearth, but her hands were shaking so badly she could not strike one. After the third try she could have sobbed with frustration.

"L-let—me . . . tr-try." Alan dropped to his knees beside her, but his hands were so stiff that the container slipped through his fingers when he tried to take it from her.

Pam shook her head adamantly, instinctively seeking the only source of heat either of them was likely to find. She wound her arms around him, tugging down the zipper of her coat and spreading it to cover them both, as she gasped, "Put—your hands under my c-coat. Got to—warm up."

He obeyed without question, pressing himself close to her body warmth and pushing his hands beneath her coat, against her back. As cold as she was, she could feel the shock of his colder hands even through her sweater.

She tugged at his blanket cape, drawing it more securely over his arms and covering her own chilled face with the folds. "If you—try anything f-funny," she added, rather belatedly, with her voice muffled in the blankets, "I'll—k-kill you."

It was a moment before he replied, through irregular, choppy breaths, "If I tried anything—funny, the effort—would probably kill me."

It was a long time before Pam could think about anything except how miserable she was. The racking shivers, the burning ache of her throat and lungs, the stiffness of her neck and limbs took precedence over whatever awkwardness she might otherwise have felt at finding herself wrapped in an intimate embrace with a stranger whose name she didn't even know.

There was certainly nothing sexy or even enjoyable about it. All she could feel were the constant, successive shudders from him that matched her own. All she could hear was his painful, staccato breathing which was occasionally punctuated by a muffled moan and all she could see were the tips of his shiny blond hair, now beginning to darken with melting snow. Pam tried to remember all she knew about hypothermia and frostbite. Sleepiness, lethargy, slurred speech...neither of them seemed to be suffering from those symptoms yet. As for frostbite—white skin, numbness...she had to check for frostbite. But she was just beginning to bring the shivers under control and she couldn't make herself move away from the meager heat his body provided just yet.

"How—do you feel?" she felt compelled to ask after a time.

His forehead was pressed against her shoulder, obviously seeking the same warmth beneath the blankets that she was, and he didn't look up to reply. "I hope you won't take this personally..." His arms tightened around her with another shiver. "But—I've had better dates."

A small sound escaped her, which could have been a laugh if she had had more strength. "So have I."

His breath was warm against the hollow of her neck, and it was heaven. She snuggled closer to fully take advantage of it. She became aware for the first time that his legs were wrapped around her thighs, and the warmth was just beginning to penetrate her jeans. That was wonderful, too.

"You weren't really..." Her words were interrupted by another ungraceful shiver, but this time the shudder was precipitated by returning warmth, not paralyzing cold. "Born in Istanbul?"

"Of course I was."

"How come?"

"My mother—was a thrill-seeker."

"To say—the least." This time she subdued the shiver by snuggling deeper into the folds of the blankets, where a nice pocket of warmth was developing between his shoulder and the curve of his elbow. "So how did you end up in California?"

"S-stupidity." He shivered violently, and Pam abandoned the warmth of the blankets to chafe his arms and shoulders with her hands.

"I'll try the fire again," she offered.

"Not yet." He drew her closer, selfishly drinking of her warmth, and Pam was glad. The space outside the circle of his arms seemed as challenging as the storm had been, and she wasn't ready to brave it again.

"This is my first blizzard," he offered after a moment.

"How do you like it so far?"

He adjusted his weight so that his legs formed a tighter circle and she was brought more securely against his chest. "It's getting better."

Pam spent a brief moment wondering whether or not that was a come-on, and debating whether she should object, then decided she didn't care. He was warm, and he was available, and though Pam had never imagined a time in her life when those would be the only prerequisites for sharing a close embrace with a man, that was the situation. All other considerations seemed petty in comparison.

Though the air around them and the floor beneath them were still icy cold and Pam could not have said she was at any time comfortable, the shared warmth made everything more bearable. Eventually she was able to focus on something besides her suffering, and her senses became alert to new impressions. The weight of his thigh across hers, the lean shape of his upper arm as it circled her back. His cheek, still

roughened and chapped from the wind, was pressed
against hers and the circle of his breath on her neck
was no longer simply pleasantly warm, but tingling,
tantalizing. She could feel his heartbeat against her
breast and the rise and fall of his chest. Her ungloved
hand was wound into the hem of his sweater for
warmth and she could feel the muscles of his back beneath the soft, cotton-knit shirt he wore, and the curve
of his spine. None of these sensations was unpleas-
ant, but they were most definitely intimate. She decided she should be disturbed by that, but made no
immediate move to do anything about it.

"Do you know," he murmured after a time, "this
is really no way for two people to behave who haven't
been properly introduced. My name's Alan Donovan."

She became aware that his shivers had long since
dissipated, and his voice had an entirely too comfortable drawl to it. Reluctantly she moved away a little,
realizing that the embrace was no longer necessary for
warmth—merely enjoyable. "Pamela Mercer," she
replied politely.

He smiled at her. "Nice to meet you, Pamela. I'd
shake your hand but mine are busy where they are."

He didn't move or try to take advantage of the situation in any way, but something about his smile made
her uncomfortable. It was a perfectly nice smile, easy
and unstrained, with the hint of a warm sparkle in the
depth of his gray eyes. But it reminded her too clearly
that he was a man, and a stranger, and this had gone
on too long.

She took his wrists and removed his hands from around her waist, saying firmly, "I'll start the fire."

The absence of his warmth was just as disagreeable as she had thought it would be and she moved quickly to strike a match to the crumpled wads of paper at the bottom of the stove. The flame caught and flared with a quick flash of heat that promised more and she gratefully pulled off her other glove and stretched her hands before it.

"You'd better check your fingers for frostbite," she advised over her shoulder, adding a little more kindling to the fire.

Alan stretched his hands out before him dubiously. "What does it look like?"

Pam reluctantly turned her back on the fire to examine his hands in the dim orange glow. They were large hands, she noticed, which she somehow hadn't expected from someone with his lean build, and despite the chapped knuckles and fingertips, quite beautiful. When she took his hands to turn them over she noticed that the palms were smooth and uncallused. His were the hands of a man with a tender touch.

She was a little embarrassed to be caught admiring his hands when she was supposed to be examining them, and she released them abruptly. "They look fine to me," she said, perhaps a little too cheerfully. "You're lucky."

She turned back to make a quick inspection of the fire, found it satisfactory, and got to her feet. "I'll have a look around. You'd better take off your wet shoes and socks. And..." She gestured toward the mantel. ''Why don't you light one of those lanterns? Every little bit of heat we can get will help.''

When she was gone, Alan pulled off his shoes and socks and lifted his feet to the hearth, massaging them to a painful restoration of circulation. The fire was beginning to catch and throw off an acceptable blanket of heat, enough at least to ease some of the ache that went right through to his bones.

Alan considered himself something of an adventurer; seeking out new and exotic experiences was his way of adding diversion to what was otherwise a very dull and staid existence. But his adventures were carefully chosen and meticulously controlled for safety and comfort, and by no stretch of the imagination could that agonizing trek up the mountain be considered a mere diversion. He wished with all his might that he had never left California.

After a moment he got up, wincing as his bare feet struck the icy floor, and hobbled over to the door where he had left his duffel bag. He rummaged around until he found a pair of socks and pulled them on, then another pair on top and another pair on top of that. He unwound the damp woolen scarf from his head and combed his fingers through his hair, but didn't discard the blankets. Then he set about trying to figure out how to light the lantern.

It was an oil lamp with a cotton wick. He had seen them before, of course, in novelty stores, but he had always assumed they were simply for decorative purposes. It looked dangerous to him. He couldn't ascertain how one was supposed to put a match to the wick without igniting the oil, and when he turned the key on the side as he had seen people do in movies, nothing happened. He had always managed to take along battery-powered lamps when tackling the great outdoors, and frontier living had never been his forte. He decided to leave the matter to Pamela, who at least appeared to know what she was doing.

There were, however, two candles on the mantel, and so as not to appear completely helpless, he lit them. They didn't offer much light, but the glow was kind of cozy, if coziness had any value at this point.

He could hear Pamela moving around in the far part of the house, but a long oak serving bar divided the room and he couldn't see her. He settled down on the hearth, drawing up his legs for further warmth, and surveyed his surroundings. *An interesting turn of events*, he mused, trying hard to keep his spirits up. *Lost in a blizzard in the Colorado Rockies, breaking into a stranger's cabin with a woman I don't even know.... Not exactly your run-of-the-mill Friday afternoon.*

This was hardly where he had expected to end up when he left California. But then, again, it was as good a place as any, he supposed. When he left California he hadn't expected anything, at all.

"No telephone," Pam announced, coming back into the room. "And the power is turned off at the source. I figured it would be—most people winterize their cabins by the first of November." She hurried forward, stretching her hands out toward the fire. "But there's an emergency generator out back, enough to run the water pump if the pipes aren't frozen. I'll start it up in a minute. And there's plenty of firewood in the shed."

Alan was becoming uneasy. "You sound like you're expecting to be here for a while."

She didn't meet his eyes. Apparently the prospect held no more appeal for her than it did for him. "The snow hasn't let up," she admitted. "If anything, it's worse. It might be a while before we can get back down to the road."

Alan released a long breath through his teeth. He couldn't explain why he found the situation so depressing. At least he was out of the snow, warm, and not dead of carbon-monoxide poisoning. But he didn't like the feeling of being trapped. He didn't like being out of control. And he just couldn't picture himself sitting here huddled over this stove doing nothing for an indeterminate amount of time. Things like this did not happen to Alan Donovan. They simply *didn't*.

"Probably somebody has found the cars," he offered confidently. "They're already looking for us."

She didn't answer, but she didn't have to. Even if someone did find the cars, how would they know where to look? With all the dozens of traffic accidents on the roads today, what would be remarkable about two more abandoned cars? And he wasn't fooling himself, not by much. He'd been out in that storm. No one would come looking for them.

"Oh, well," he mumbled, "at least I didn't have any plans for the weekend."

"It might let up," she suggested, but he could see it was a forced hope. "Probably in no more than an hour or two. We can hike down to the highway and get help.''

But Alan couldn't see himself hiking anywhere in that snow, not ever again. In fact, the more he thought over the situation, the more grim it became, until he decided the best thing to do was not to think about it at all. Nothing good ever came of imagining the worst.

"Well, we might as well make the best of it," he offered philosophically. "Why don't we start by opening up those shutters? It's as gloomy as a tomb in here."

"In the middle of this storm?" she replied impatiently. "If I'm not mistaken, that's what *storm* shutters are for."

"Oh." He was silent for a moment. "What about candles? Did you find any more of those?"

"I'm sure Mr. McMurty has a store of them around here some place." She glanced at the two burning on the mantel. "Why didn't you light the lantern?"

"I couldn't figure out how it worked."

She gave him an odd look, then took the lantern down from the mantel. She removed the globe, struck a match to the wick, and it caught instantly. When she replaced the globe, she turned the key on the side—it worked for her—and the flame grew to a gentle glow that illuminated half the room. "It's really not all that hard," she said.

Alan shrugged. "Where I come from, we press a switch on the wall. Just a matter of technique, I guess."

She murmured, "I guess." And she reached forward and closed the stove doors on the crackling blaze.

"What are you doing that for?" he objected. "We'll freeze."

"The room will heat much faster with the doors closed," she explained, adjusting the vents. "It's a radiant-heat stove."

That violated every scientific principle Alan had ever heard of, and he didn't believe it for a minute. But after his incompetence with the lantern he didn't feel inclined to argue with her. She would find out for herself when icicles started to form on the furniture.

She zipped up her coat and pulled on her gloves again. "I guess I'd better go start the generator."

"Do you need any help?"

"Do you know anything about gasoline-powered generators?"

"No," he admitted. "But I'll be happy to supervise."

She smiled dryly as she turned to leave the room. "Thanks, anyway."

Another man would have felt awkward, resting himself in front of the fire while she took over, but not Alan. For one thing, he was still too cold to feel much of anything. For another, he was accustomed to others doing things for him. It wasn't a sign of laziness or even selfishness. That was simply the way things were.

But she was gone for quite some time, and as the stove—against all logic—began to warm the room to the point that sitting near it became uncomfortable, her industriousness touched a chord of guilt within

Alan. He got up, untied the blankets from around his shoulders, and thought the least he could do, if they were going to be here for a while, was try to make the place habitable.

He removed the dust covers one by one, folding them into a neat pile, feeling somewhat like a burglar as he did so. He wondered if there was any chance the owner of the cabin might return, and dismissed the possibility immediately. Nobody went to the trouble of winterizing his home only to return to it in the middle of a blizzard.

He uncovered a tufted leather sofa, some polished pine tables and a couple of sturdy, oak rocking chairs. The bed was a carved wood four-poster that looked like an antique. On the built-in shelves that lined one wall he discovered some board games, a collection of books—mostly Louis L'Amour and John Jakes—and a television set and VCR. Automatically he pushed the "on" button on the television, then remembered with a sigh that there was no power. That was too bad. The VCR, and the collection of movies he saw neatly arranged in a display case beneath it, would have made the time pass a great deal faster. What did people do, he wondered, without television?

Then he realized unhappily that he was about to find out.

He heard a faraway mechanical hum, and a few seconds later the back door opened on a cold gust of air. "I got it started," she announced, rubbing her hands vigorously together as she went over to the kitchen sink. "Now, let's just see if it did any good...."

She turned on the faucet and for the longest time there was nothing but a disappointing gurgling and sputtering of air. Then at last the faucet spewed out a gush of clear water, and Pamela congratulated herself with a laugh.

"You sure do know how to do some interesting things," Alan said admiringly.

She glanced at him as though uncertain whether or not he was mocking her, then shrugged. "Unfortunately, we don't have enough electricity for hot water, but this is better than nothing, I suppose."

She began opening cabinet doors. "Well, at least we won't starve . . . not if you're into SpaghettiOs and Roller Coasters, that is. Mr. McMurty must have the taste buds of a three-year-old."

The way she was taking inventory of the food supply indicated to Alan again that she expected to be here much longer than he intended to, and once again he was depressed. "Any chocolate?" he inquired.

She shook her head. "Here's some coffee, though."

Alan made an effort to get into the spirit of things. "Good enough. Where's the percolator?"

She snapped open the canister top and sniffed the aroma of the coffee appreciatively. "I told you, there's not enough electricity for appliances."

"Great." Alan tried not to be annoyed. "We've got coffee, but we can't make it. That's like being locked in a warehouse full of soup without a can opener."

She chuckled, looking through the bottom cabinets. "Not quite. We'll just do it the old-fashioned way."

"How?"

She brought up a metal pot. "Boil it on the stove."

Alan watched her fill the pot with water, and scoop the coffee grounds directly into it. "Do you know how some people fantasize about going back to nature?" he commented after a moment. "I'm not one of them."

She spared him a single noncommittal glance and took the pot to the stove.

"You don't really mind, do you?" he inquired, following her.

She set the pot on top of the stove. "Mind what?"

"Everything." He made an all-inclusive gesture. "I mean, it was really nice of you to save my life, but doesn't it bother you, being stuck up here for who-knows-how-long with a complete stranger you picked up on the side of the road? I could be an ax-murderer or a rapist or a crazed drug dealer."

She hesitated, appearing to consider this for the first time. Alan noticed that her eyes were a deep, clear green, and her skin, now that it was losing some of the rawness of the bitter cold and taking on a glow from the stove, was an appealing blend of peaches and cream.

"Are you?" she demanded simply.

He blinked. "Well, no. But—"

"There, you see." She turned back to make a minute adjustment on the stove vent. "The fact is, most folks are pretty ordinary when you come right down to it. It's only the news reports that make people want to jump at shadows."

Alan was somewhat amazed. He wasn't certain he had ever met anyone who was that gullible, and so unabashedly honest about it. She grew more intriguing by the minute. First, she saved him from a certain death by carbon-monoxide poisoning and/or freezing, led the way unfalteringly through a blizzard to shelter, then she provided heat, light and water under conditions so rustic they would have baffled Davy Crockett, and she even knew how to make coffee without a percolator. It appeared that nothing daunted her, not even the prospect of being isolated in this remote mountain spot with a strange man and not even a telephone to call for help. Alan supposed that he should find all that competence intimidating, but in fact he admired it.

He shook his head with a little grin. "I guess you're what they call a genuine hero, aren't you?"

Again, she looked as though she did not quite know how to take that. Then she inquired curiously, "So. If you're not an ax-murderer or a rapist or a drug dealer, what are you?"

He chuckled. "Not a hero, that's for sure."

She dragged a rocking chair closer to the stove. "No, I mean what do you do?"

He pulled the other rocking chair forward. "As little as possible."

She removed her coat and hung it on the back of the chair. For the first time Alan had a chance to notice what she looked like without her bulky overclothing, without the pinched, chapped look of cold about her, and he was pleasantly surprised. Her hair was long and dark, and she wore it in a thick braid that started at the crown of her head and ended below her shoulder blades. A feathering of bangs fell across her forehead. Nicely rounded hips were encased in light blue denim, and the plump, not overly full shape of her breasts was outlined by a dark blue mohair sweater. She wasn't fashion-model thin, like most of the women Alan knew, and he liked that.

The girl next door, he decided. That was what she looked like. Of course he had never lived in one place long enough to get to know the girl next door, so he couldn't say for certain what one was supposed to look like, but Pamela Mercer seemed to have all the qualifications. Wholesome, down-to-earth, resourceful and pretty in a well-scrubbed, no-nonsense way. Alan found all new experiences stimulating, and meeting a woman like Pamela was definitely a new experience for him. Although, given his choice in the matter he would have preferred not to risk his life in a blizzard simply to meet a woman, however unusual she might be.

Another attribute he found unusual was her persistence. "Everyone does *something*," she pointed out, a trifle impatiently. "For a living, I mean."

He shrugged. "I don't."

The look she gave him made him feel defensive, as though he should apologize for the truth. And then he was annoyed with himself for ever raising the subject of what kind of man she might have condemned herself to weather out the storm with, because once her curiosity was roused she did not appear to have any intention of letting the matter drop.

"Are you independently wealthy or something?"

"Or something." He was becoming uncomfortable, and changed the subject. "Listen, do you think it's right for us to be breaking into this man's house and using up his supplies like this? Won't he mind?"

"We didn't break in," she corrected. "We used the key. As for the supplies, that's what they're here for."

"In case someone breaks into his house and gets hungry," Alan said dryly.

"Sure." She seemed perfectly serious. "When you build a place this high up, you think about things like that."

"I guess this McMurty fellow is a friend of yours, then. That's how you knew where the key was."

"Not exactly." She leaned forward to make another adjustment to the stove vent. "But I've been up here with my dad a few times when he made his rounds. He's the sheriff around here."

Alan stared at her. "Your father is a sheriff?"

"That's right."

Alan began to laugh, slowly and softly. There was nothing else he could do. "The sheriff," he repeated, and shook his head in absolute disbelief over the way his luck was running.

Her brows drew together uncertainly. "What's funny about that?"

"Nothing," he assured her, making an effort to bring his mirth under control. "Nothing except that— I've been sitting here thinking about how great it's going to be when someone rescues us, and I just figured out that the person who'll probably be doing the rescuing is your father. The sheriff. And I'm wanted by the law."

Three

___

For a long time Pam said nothing. She simply looked at him, her eyes unblinking and her expression unchanged. Then she cleared her throat a little and inquired, "For what?"

Alan hesitated, then grimaced, pushing his hair back with his fingers. "It's a long, boring story. You wouldn't be interested."

She didn't remove her gaze from his face, although there was definitely a trace of wariness there now. And her tone was humorless as she assured him, "Trust me. I'm interested."

The truth was, Pam wasn't nearly as gullible as she appeared. Growing up in a rural community had shielded her from some of the realities of urban life, and it was true her experience had taught her that most people were not so different from herself and that, given a chance, a basic goodness would emerge in almost everyone. But she wasn't stupid; her father was a law officer and there were dangers in the world for which one could not always be prepared. It was rather unsettling to find herself now seated only a few feet away from one of those dangers.

In the few seconds that passed Pam found herself quickly assessing her situation and devising defenses against it—which were pitifully few—and at the same time assuring herself of what she already knew: this man was not dangerous. No one who was foolish enough to barricade himself in a snow-locked car with the heater running or brave a Colorado winter without a coat could possibly present a danger to anyone but himself. Besides, she remembered the way he had looked, frozen and miserable on the trek up here but bravely making jokes, and the way they had clung to each other for warmth.... She simply could not have been that close to a dangerous criminal without knowing it. But still...

Seeing the trepidation on her face, Alan immediately assured her, "Don't worry. I didn't kill anyone or anything."

"That's a relief." But her expression was still cautious, and more than a little curious.

Sighing, Alan saw no way out of it but to tell the truth, ridiculous though he knew it would sound. "I had a fight with my father," he admitted, "and stormed out of the house—taking his Porsche with me. I was pulled over for speeding in Nevada and found out he'd reported the car stolen. When the officer tried to take me in, I was so mad—I just drove off. Not many police cars can catch a Porsche in high gear,'' he explained to her simply. And then he shook his head and avoided her eyes. "I've never done anything like that in my life," he finished softly.

He looked so genuinely embarrassed and miserable that Pam wanted to laugh out loud with relief. Not that grand theft and resisting arrest were laughing matters, by any means, it was simply that no one who was that contrite could possibly be considered a hardened criminal.

She couldn't keep a hint of amusement out of her tone as she suggested, "Aren't you a little old to be running away from home?"

A touch of dry humor turned up his mouth at one corner. "First you've got to have a home to run away from."

That, Pam suspected, was the long story. And though she was unabashedly curious, she could see that the subject was making him uncomfortable and she decided not to pry—for the moment. At the very least, they would be stuck together for several hours, and there was no reason to start out by offending him.

She lifted her shoulders philosophically. "Oh, well, I wouldn't worry about it too much. Not too many people go to jail for a traffic violation. Besides, they can't arrest you if they can't find you, can they?"

Alan's lips curved into a slow smile that gradually sparked a light of appreciation in his eyes. "I knew there was a bright side."

Watching him smile, seeing the way his eyes lit up
with a kind of lazy warmth from deep within that
slowly spread across his face, Pam knew that she
hadn't been mistaken in her first impression about
him. Had he just confessed to being Charlie Manson
in disguise she would have shrugged it off without a
qualm because everything about him stated quietly
and clearly that whatever else he might be, he
was . . . well, *nice*.

Pam had never boasted of being a particularly good
judge of character—if she had been, she would have
had Peter pegged long ago—but she had no doubts
about Alan Donovan. His was the kind of face that
could keep few secrets and would lie with difficulty, if
at all. True, even without the Porsche and the claim
that he did nothing at all for a living, there was a sug-
gestion of elitism about him, and even on first glance
Pam had been able to tell that he came from a different world than most men she met. But beneath it all
there was a simple, common decency that was impossible to disguise, and Pam felt comfortable with him.
When he smiled, she wanted to smile back. She decided right then and there that she liked him.

The smile lingered, in his eyes as well as hers, and
Pam became aware that he was looking at her with the
same sort of gentle assessment she was regarding him
with. And then he said, without warning, "You're
pretty."

The compliment unsettled her, both because it was
unexpected and because he said it with such plain,
unplanned sincerity. She blinked with surprise, and
felt color tingle in her cheeks. "Thank you," she said,

and turned her attention to the stove. What she really wanted to do was return the compliment, but she found herself saying instead, perhaps a little too hastily, "The coffee smells like it's about done. I'll get the cups."

Alan's smile was shadowed with puzzlement as he watched her go. It was a cliché but true: it had been a long time since he had seen a woman blush like that. He supposed if more women knew how enchanting a blush could be, they would do it more often—but he didn't imagine any of them could do it as nicely, as gracefully, as she did. And then he was disturbed. He hoped she didn't think he was coming on to her.

Which brought up an interesting question. Was he?

The answer to that had to be an unqualified *No*. There was a time and a place for everything, and this most definitely was neither. They had bigger things to worry about, and he was on shaky ground with her as it was, considering the confession he had just made to her about his peccadillo with the police. She had every right to be suspicious of him, and he would be an imbecile to complicate the situation. There was no point in making things more uncomfortable than they already were, for either of them.

So, when she returned, he did the only rational thing. He apologized. "I didn't mean to embarrass you a minute ago. Sometimes I talk before I think."

Her eyes widened. "You mean you don't think I'm pretty?"

"Well, yes." He was taken aback. "I mean, no. What I mean is, of course I think you're pretty. I wouldn't have said so if I didn't."

"Good." The edges of an impish grin twitched at her lips. "Because I think you are, too."

Alan laughed. He was beginning to like her more and more.

She poured the coffee through a tea strainer into two mugs, and handed him one. It was steaming, black and ugly-looking. Despite the tea strainer, bits of coffee grounds floated on top. He looked at it dubiously. "No cream, I suppose."

Her returned glance was dry. "You suppose right."

She resumed her seat in the rocking chair, cradling her cup carefully in both hands as she tucked one foot beneath her. She looked at him with a frank, cheerfully curious expression and invited, "Tell me about yourself."

"What do you want to know?"

"Everything."

He chuckled. "That could take some time."

She gestured around the empty cabin. "I would say we have plenty of that."

Alan didn't know where to begin. He wasn't accustomed to talking about himself and he had never met anyone who was interested enough to inquire in any but the most superficial way. And the worst thing was, though he generally considered himself to be a good conversationalist, he could not think of a single thing to say that would interest her.

He grinned a little, and shook his head. "Sorry. I guess I never realized before how boring I am."

"A man who was born in Istanbul cannot be boring," she pointed out. "Start there."

"I don't remember much about it." And at her look of impatience he grinned again and amended, "My father was working in the Middle East and my mother, for some reason or another, decided to go with him. When it came time for me to enter the world the nearest medical facilities were in Istanbul. We flew home two weeks later."

So far, she didn't look bored, so he went on, "For a while I lived with my grandparents in Michigan, and then my mother went to New York."

"What about your father?"

"He was a jerk, so she left him." He took a small sip of the coffee and tried not to grimace. "He made up for it later, though, with enormously substantial alimony payments."

"Is your father rich?" she asked guilelessly.

Alan nodded, appearing to be neither surprised nor offended by the personal nature of her question. "Very. At last count, number twenty on the list of the wealthiest men in the nation."

"Oh." She studied him carefully, looking for telltale signs of his exclusive status . . . and finding them, naturally. They were subtle, but unmistakable: the faint trace of an Ivy League accent, the flawless styling of his hair, the custom fit of his clothes, even the way he held his shoulders and moved his hands—all spoke of a culture and a background that was very far removed from anything she had ever known. And it fascinated her. "Now, *that's* interesting."

"No," he corrected. His eyes were on his cup. "That's impressive. There's a difference."

Though Pamela could not possibly relate to the sensation, she had to wonder what it was like, being the son of one of the wealthiest men in America. The experiences he must have had, the people he knew, the places he had seen, the life-style he lead . . . This *was* exciting. She wanted to ask a dozen questions, but something about his face made her hesitate. Perhaps being one of the very rich was not as pleasant as she imagined.

She said, "The top twenty, huh? I'd be happy to be in the top one thousand."

Alan shrugged and took another sip of his coffee. This time he made a face. "God, this stuff is foul. Is there any sugar?"

"No." She hesitated, then ventured, "I guess—you get tired of people making a fuss about your father."

He sighed. "And comparing me to my father, and recognizing me because of my father, and using me to get to my father. Sometimes I feel like I'm nothing but an extension of my father, and I barely know the man."

All of that was said without bitterness or rancor, but there was something so bleak in the simple statement of fact that Pam's heart twisted. "Was it very hard—growing up with him?"

He looked surprised. "I didn't grow up with him. I was in private schools by the time I was six. I was raised by nuns."

She couldn't help smiling. "*That's* interesting, too. I've never known anyone who was raised by nuns before."

"Haven't you? I know lots."

Different worlds, Pam thought, somewhat dazed. She inquired, "What about your mother?"

"She married an Italian fashion designer."

"*Fashion* designer?"

Alan grinned. "Yeah, I know. I thought they were all gay, too. But this one's not. Then again, he's not very successful, either." He shrugged and took another reluctant sip of his coffee. "Anyway, I still see her sometimes, but I don't like her husband much."

Pam shook her head slowly. "What a strange life you must have had."

He appeared to think about that for a minute. "Not strange," he decided. "Just...life."

"So," she said lightly, trying to be sophisticated, "I guess this makes you an international playboy, doesn't it? I've never met one of those before."

He laughed, his eyes twinkling with silver sparks that Pam found enchanting to watch. "Sorry to disappoint you, but you still haven't."

She shook her head reprovingly. "Shame on you. Don't you know you have an image to maintain? Wild parties, private jets, sex, drugs, and rock and roll—the whole bit."

His eyes were amused. "It sounds like you've been watching too much television. Playboys are people, too, you know."

She smiled, her mind on a dozen other questions she wanted to ask him. If Pam had an overwhelming weakness, it was her curiosity—about people, events, in fact everything around her, but especially about people. Alan Donovan was without a doubt the most unusual person she had ever met or was likely to meet, and she wanted to know every detail, to store up memories of this exotic encounter against the long dull months and years ahead.

She said, "But what do you—" And then she caught herself. How many times had her mother pointed out to her that there was a fine line between polite curiosity and downright prying? Some people didn't enjoy having their lives spread open and dissected for the sake of a virtual stranger's satisfaction.

"Sorry," she apologized with a rueful smile. "I guess I'm starting to sound like an interviewer. I don't mean to make you uncomfortable."

"You're not." The statement seemed to surprise Alan as much as it did her, as he added, "You're easy to talk to. I don't know many people I can just talk to." And then he smiled. "I'm glad I met you, Pamela Mercer."

She liked the way he said that, slowly and thoughtfully, with just a hint of cautious puzzlement, as if it were a truth that took some getting used to. And the way he looked at her when he said it, with a kind of gentle musing, made her skin tingle again with pleasure.

She said, "Most people call me Pam."

"I like Pamela," he responded immediately. "It sounds like it belongs to a character in a costume drama. Lady Pamela. It suits you."

She made a face. "I hate that name. Nobody ever uses it except my mother when she's mad at me."

"Well, I'm not your mother and I'm not mad at you, but I'm going to call you Pamela." He lifted his cup again. "What difference can it make for a few hours? After we get out of here you'll never have to hear 'Pamela' again—except from an angry mother,'' he added with a grin.

She gave him a wry look. "You can be pretty autocratic for someone who doesn't even know how to light an oil lamp."

"I can't know everything," he pointed out. "Do *you* know how to get away from a charging rhinoceros who's trying to protect her young?"

Pamela's eyes widened. "No. How?"

"Run," he replied, deadpan.

She laughed. He *was* fun, in an offbeat kind of way. If she had to be stranded in a snowstorm, she certainly could have chosen worse companions, even if he did insist upon calling her Pamela. And, on top of everything else, he was extremely pleasant to look at, and she liked his smile.

She tilted her head toward him curiously and inquired, "Is that your real hair color?"

Alan looked momentarily taken aback. "Yes."

"It doesn't look like it."

"Is that good or bad?"

"Good, I think."

"Why, thank you."

And then she saw the subtle teasing light in his eyes and she blushed. Despite all he'd told her about his background, it was easy to forget he was much more sophisticated than she was. He probably thought she was flirting with him, and was enjoying every moment of it. Pam wasn't used to guarding her thoughts or her actions, but it was clear that with a man like Alan Donovan she would have to be more careful.

She got up quickly and went to the door, opening it a fraction. A gust of arctic air and a blur of snow greeted her, and she closed the door firmly. "It doesn't look like it's letting up any," she announced dolefully.

He turned in his chair, his brow creased with a frown of concern. "Don't you have anybody who'll be wondering where you are?"

Pam sighed. Normally, she would have had three households of overprotective family members frantically calling each other trying to locate her, but this weekend... "Not really. My folks were kind of expecting me to be away for the weekend."

"Great." His tone was heavy. "We're probably the only two people in the whole state who are *not* expected home for dinner. It could be days before anyone misses us."

She had no easy rejoinder for that.

Seeing the look of dejection on her face depressed Alan alarmingly, so he quickly changed the subject. "Where were you going this weekend?"

"No place important."

Alan was confused when her expression changed from sad to bleak. That was not at all what he had intended.

"Anyway," she added with a shrug, "I finished early."

"It must have been pretty important," he ventured, "to bring you out in this weather."

She went over to the shelves on the far wall and began to thumb through the titles. "I was meeting a friend at the airport. He decided not to stay."

From the flat, almost too-casual manner in which that statement was delivered Alan could perceive several things: tension, unhappiness and embarrassment were among them. "Boyfriend," he deduced out loud.

"Fiancé." She didn't turn, but selected a book. "Ex-fiancé, I should say. He found someone he liked better."

"He told you that at the *airport*?" Alan couldn't keep a note of incredulity out of his voice.

She turned, holding the book in her hand, her expression mildly defensive. "Well, what else could he do? He had to tell me sometime."

Alan tried hard to sound noncommittal, but it wasn't easy. "And you don't mind?"

"Why should I?" There was definitely a trace of defiance in her eyes now. "It was just one of those things. We were never very well matched."

"You're not upset about it, at all? Not even the least bit angry?"

"Why should I be? He's a very nice man, and I wish him the best."

She sounded perfectly sincere—in fact, too sincere. Although he knew it was none of his business, Alan couldn't help remarking, "He sounds like a jerk to me."

She lifted her chin, her eyes growing cool. "I hardly think you're in a position to judge."

Alan accepted the reprimand in silence, but his opinion didn't change. It *was* none of his business, but when a man broke off an engagement between plane changes—probably on his way to the other woman— it seemed plain to Alan that the man couldn't be anything else but a jerk. And when a man broke off an engagement to a woman as pretty, and as nice, as Pamela Mercer, it was also apparent that he was stupid. She was obviously better off without him.

But he didn't like to think about her being treated that way. And when he considered what she had been through today—dumped by a lover, wrecking her car, being stranded in a blizzard—his admiration for her, and his confusion about her, grew. And he found, much to his surprise, that he couldn't remain impartial on the subject. Nor could he stay silent.

"You must not think very much of yourself, to let somebody treat you like that and not even get *mad* about it."

"There's nothing to be mad about, I told you." Her voice was sharp and she was dismayed by her own lack of patience. After all, it was she who had opened the field for personal observations with her intense questioning of him, and she could hardly be annoyed with him for following her lead. But she was. "Anyway, it's none of your business and I don't want to talk about it."

"I think you should talk to somebody," he replied, completely unfazed, "and you've got a captive audience."

Pam opened her mouth for a sharp retort, but caught herself in time. "There's nothing to talk about," she replied, forcing evenness into her tone. "And anyway, I don't even know you."

Alan's silence reminded her pointedly that he had told her things he probably wouldn't have shared with a complete stranger under normal circumstances, and she felt small. Then she realized that that was it—the circumstances. Here they were, strangers who never should have met, trapped together for an unknown period of time, both of them scared and trying not to show it; naturally they would behave in ways they ordinarily wouldn't. But a line had to be drawn somewhere. This could get out of hand.

She released a thoughtful breath. "Look," she said carefully, "this cabin can get awfully small if we don't watch ourselves. I know I was a little pushy earlier, and I'm sorry, but the thing is we've got to respect each other's privacy. I mean, if we were at a party or something we wouldn't be prying into each other's personal lives like this. Think about it like that."

"If we were at a party," he commented with a disparaging glance at his coffee cup, "I'd be drinking champagne instead of mud and it wouldn't make much difference what we talked about."

If we were at a party, Pam thought, *he never would have noticed me . . . not that I'd be likely to be at the kind of party he attends, anyway.* There was something very telling about that, and only another good reason for keeping her distance.

Alan set his mug on the hearth and folded his hands across his middle, regarding her with a frank, unwavering gaze which made her rather nervous. "I don't like your party theory," he decided at last. "As a matter of fact, I don't like parties, at all, which is why I almost never go to them."

"Well, think about it however you want," she replied, hugging her book to her chest. "All I'm saying is this will be a lot easier if we give each other some space.''

"The Twilight Zone," he said, and a startled laugh escaped her.

"What?"

"This is more like the Twilight Zone than a party," he explained reasonably. "You know, a world of shadow and substance, where nothing is quite what it seems. You're not taking proper advantage of this situation, Pamela Mercer.''

She looked at Alan, so lean and sexy with his long legs stretched out before him and his eyes twinkling playfully, and she realized that was exactly what she was afraid of: the very definite temptation to take advantage of the situation.

"This is the Great Escape," he went on easily. "Nobody knows where we are, nobody expects anything from us, even *we* don't know anything about each other—so for a few hours we can just relax and be whatever we want to be.''

"Like what?" she said cautiously.

"Well…" He gave her an odd, almost hesitant look. "We could be friends.''

Pamela relaxed. "Okay," she agreed immediately. "Friends. *Polite* friends," she added pointedly.

"Who don't ask personal questions about each other.''

"Right.''

"A friend should be allowed to say whatever is on his mind," he pointed out.

"And a friend should also be allowed to refuse to answer."

"You don't want to talk about your ex-boyfriend."

"Right."

Alan shook his head. "It could be a long afternoon."

"Not for me." She held up the book.

"What am I supposed to do?"

Pamela settled down on the sofa and opened her book. "There are plenty of other books on the shelves."

"I don't like Westerns."

Pamela's lips tightened ruefully. Another thing they didn't have in common.

"Then watch TV."

"Very funny."

"You could always just sit and listen to the snow fall."

He started to reply, but she turned a page of the book and he realized she was no longer listening. After a moment he got up and walked over to the bookshelves, but found only what he already knew—there was nothing there he wanted to read. Alan decided to explore the cabin, and that took about two minutes. It was strange: he had spent most of his life doing nothing, but now, faced with the prospect of nothing to do, he didn't think he could stand it. Especially, he realized, since all he really wanted to do was talk to Pamela.

But she was completely immersed in her book, and he was left to fend for himself. He stole a glance at her,

her profile shadowed by the glow of the candle, one shapely denim-encased leg propped up on the arm of the sofa as she half-reclined against the cushions, her sweater molding the shape of her breasts. He sighed.

It was definitely going to be a long afternoon.

Four

2:05 p.m.

I am going out of my mind!'' Alan gestured dramatically and paced to the shuttered window. "If we don't get out of here soon I'm going to run screaming out into the snow. I can't stay locked up in here, you don't understand, I've got to have something to *do*. People weren't meant to be locked up, they go crazy."

Pam calmly turned a page of her book and he whirled on her. "It's cabin fever," he declared. "I saw a movie once about a guy who got cabin fever and carved up his whole family. That's what happens when people are locked up too long."

"You don't have cabin fever," Pam replied absently. "We've only been here a little over an hour."

"An hour, a day, what does it matter when you're locked up in the dark with nothing to do but listen to your hair grow? Are you sure we can't open the shutters?"

"I'm sure. Maybe you should think of this as practice."

"For what?"

She did not look up from the book. "Well, for a man in your precarious position with the law, it might not hurt you to get used to the idea of being locked up."

Alan glared at her. "I thought you said I wouldn't go to jail."

She shrugged and turned another page. "I'm not a judge."

He began to pace again. "Well, at least in jail there's something to *do*," he muttered. "They have television in jail, don't they? And arts and crafts? Maybe I could take up woodworking."

"I think you have jail confused with summer camp."

"Do you want to play a game?"

"I'm reading."

"Checkers? Charades?"

"Oh, for heaven's sake, will you calm down?" She turned another page. "You're as bad as my kids."

He stopped, and stared at her. "Kids? You didn't tell me you had children."

Pam noted his expression out of the corner of her eye but kept her own face blank, her attention focused on the book. "No, I guess I didn't."

Alan continued to look at her oddly. "Kids? More than one?"

She fought against the small smile that tugged at the corner of her lips. "Um-hm. Fifteen to be exact, all under the age of five."

She looked up at him, grinning. "I teach preschool." She tossed the book aside and stood. "So, you see I have a lot of experience taking care of cranky little boys. You have your choice: food or a nap. One of them always works."

A playful sparkle came into Alan's eyes and he gave her a lopsided grin that reminded her he could in no way be considered a little boy. "Will you tell me a bedtime story?" he suggested.

She regarded him thoughtfully. "Somehow I think you're a little old for bedtime stories."

He sighed. "Aren't we all?"

Pam was certain there was a double meaning there, but preferred not to spend time pondering it. "I think we'd better have lunch," she decided.

She went into the kitchen and he followed. "Well, what'll it be?" she said, opening the cabinet. "SpaghettiOs or Roller Coasters?"

"Beef stroganoff."

"With a fresh tossed salad and a dry red wine?"

"And peach melba for dessert."

He leaned over her shoulder, pushing aside cans and freeze-dried food packets as Pam tried to see what was available. The faintest hint of an early-morning cologne still clung to him; it was a subtle, elusive scent that made Pam wish he would stand closer so she could determine what the fragrance was.

"The owner of this place must have been storing up for a nuclear holocaust," he muttered as a stack of tuna fish tumbled over beneath his impatient search.

"Lucky for us. Look, you're making a mess. Just go sit down and let me— Eureka! Beef stew! Not exactly stroganoff, but better than a can of spaghetti any day." She grabbed the can and turned, and found herself in the circle of his arms.

Alan's hands were still on the cabinet, his arms slightly upraised on either side of her. He was so close that her breasts brushed his chest, and when she looked up her slightly parted lips almost touched his chin. Their eyes caught and locked in mutual surprise and for a moment neither of them moved.

His scent was that of forest rain, earthy and herbal and faintly intoxicating. The warmth of his body caused her skin to tingle with reciprocal heat, and she could feel his half-released breath flutter across her cheek. And when she looked into his eyes she found herself wondering—for a brief, unwarranted and unpredictable moment—what his kiss would taste like. And she knew he was thinking the same thing.

Alan lowered his hands slowly to her shoulders, where they touched very lightly for a moment then moved away, gliding to a more natural resting position at her waist. She thought he would step away, and perhaps that was his first intention. But she could see the changing emotions on his face as clearly as flashes of light and shadow—uncertainty, hunger, hesitance, desire—and he didn't move away.

Pam didn't move, either, though she told herself it was because her backside was already pressed against the counter and there was no place to go. The truth was, she was mesmerized by expectation: his hands on her waist were broad and strong, his thighs pressed ever so lightly against hers, and his eyes, as they traveled from her lips, down her body and then to her lips again, set off little sparks of excitement in her that caused her pulse to catch painfully.

They seemed to hover forever on the edge of a promise, but in fact the insanity only lasted a few seconds. And that was exactly what it was: insanity. Pam recovered herself forcefully, gave what she hoped was the semblance of a smile, and gestured awkwardly with the can. "I guess I'd better heat this up."

Was that relief that flickered across his eyes, or regret? "Yes, I guess you'd better," he agreed. His voice sounded perfectly normal, but he did not remove his hands immediately. And there was no mistaking what was in his eyes as they moved over her face one more time. It was regret, liberally laced with wanting. And once again Pam held her breath.

When Alan lifted his eyes to hers again, it was with a forced smile and a hint of apology. He took a small step backward, letting his hands drop. "Look," he said simply, "there's no point in pretending I don't find you attractive."

For the first time, Pam breathed free. *Good*, she thought. *This is the best way to handle it. Just get it up front, talk about it, and it will go away.* But her heart was beating far too fast, and she had to clear her throat before she could speak.

"Yes, well. That's to be expected, I suppose. You're a good-looking man. It's only natural that we should be . . . attracted to one another."

"Of course, we'd be foolish to do anything about it." He was watching her closely.

"Of course," she agreed quickly.

"I mean, we don't even know each other. And just because we happen to be alone together, miles away from civilization, with no sign of rescue in sight, doesn't mean we have to—"

"No, of course not. Just because a man and a woman are alone together doesn't mean they automatically have to—"

"Exactly. People should be more responsible than that."

"The world would be a lot better place today if they were."

"Besides, you've just broken up with your fiancé and you have a lot on your mind—"

"We both do. I mean, these are not exactly ordinary circumstances—"

"Sure," he agreed, far too readily to be convincing. "It's just stress, you know. You're probably not that attractive, at all."

"And you're probably very ordinary-looking."

"Well," he said, and the beginnings of a smile made its way to his eyes. "I'm glad we got that straightened out."

"Me, too." But she found it entirely too difficult to break away from the smile in his eyes, and somehow she didn't feel the matter was resolved.

"I'll make lunch," she said, and moved quickly past him.

Though he did nothing but lean against the counter and watch, he seemed to fill up the kitchen as Pam went about preparing their lunch. She was sure that she only imagined his eyes were on the curve of her rear when she bent over to search for the pot, and there was no reason to think he was paying particular attention to the movements of her arms and the profile of her breasts as she worked the can opener. After all, they were two mature adults who had recognized the problem and dealt with it reasonably. There was nothing to be awkward about.

"Why don't you see if you can find some crackers or something?" she suggested as she took the pot over to the Franklin stove, and she was relieved when Alan turned to do something other than watch her.

She had to admire his self-discipline. There were not many men who would pause to think about responsibility when a sexual opportunity presented itself nor allow better judgment to overcome impulse. That showed a lot of character, she decided. One had to respect that.

On the other hand, this was a man who could probably have any woman he wanted with a snap of his fingers. What would he want with her? One did not have to be very noble to turn down sardines when caviar was available.

Not that it mattered, of course. The important thing was that she didn't have to worry about awkward scenes or embarrassing advances. They should both be more comfortable from now on. The subject was closed and need never be raised again.

Thus resolved, it was only reasonable that the first thing she should ask him as they sat down to beef stew and saltine crackers was, "Do you have a girlfriend?"

He picked up his spoon. "No."

"Why not?"

"I don't know." He tasted the stew and made a face. "This stuff is really awful."

Pam sighed. "There goes your reputation again."

At his questioning look she explained, "Your international-playboy reputation. You're supposed to have dozens of girlfriends dripping in jewels and swarming all over your yacht and lounging in the plush velvet interior of the bedroom on your private jet. Couldn't you, just once, be just a little bit like what I expect? Even if you have to lie."

Alan laughed. "All right, I confess. I not only have a girlfriend, but a wife. Two wives. Three girlfriends. All of them anorexic love slaves in diamond chokers and mink bikinis. You know what this needs?" He tasted the stew again. "Wine. Excuse me."

He left the table to search through the cabinets for wine, and Pam informed him over her shoulder, "Mr. McMurty is a staunch Southern Baptist. You won't find any alcohol on the premises."

"Mr. McMurty is also..." Alan returned to the table, brandishing a bottle of California red, "a secret tippler. There are three more bottles of this stuff in the back of the cabinet, and a fifth of brandy."

Pam lifted an eyebrow. "Well, well. The things you learn when you break into a man's house."

He hesitated. "Do you think he'll mind if we drink it?"

"Heavens, no. We're saving him from himself."

"Good." He put the bottle on the table and went for glasses. "By the time we work our way through four bottles of this stuff I guess it won't matter how deep the snow gets. We'll pay him back, of course," he added.

Pam shook her head, grinning. "You're funny. You could buy the whole side of this mountain if you wanted to, and you're worried about a bottle of wine. How'd you ever get so ethical?"

"Nuns, remember?"

He returned to the table and Pam watched as he poured a liberal dollop of wine into his stew. She covered her bowl protectively as he offered to do the same for hers. "I thought you were going to drink it," she said, trying to mask her distaste.

"That, too. All the great chefs of Europe add a little wine to their beef stew. It brings out the flavor." He stirred the concoction in the bowl and tasted it. He looked disappointed. "Of course, it helps if there's some flavor to bring out. I guess the manufacturer of canned beef stew can't be expected to know anything about the great chefs of Europe."

"Do you spend a lot of time there?" Pam asked, a little eagerly. "In Europe?"

"Not really." He poured two glasses of wine. "I know just enough German and Italian to get my face slapped in two languages, and I never can figure out the currency exchange. It's easier to stay home.''

"You are the most disappointing playboy I've ever met," Pam said impatiently. "Of course," she added, "you're the only playboy I've ever met."

"I told you, I'm not a playboy."

"What *are* you then?"

Alan thought about that for a moment. "Lazy?"

"Is that how you learned what it takes to outsmart a charging rhinoceros?"

"Oh, that." He shrugged. "I do have some hobbies."

Pam supposed that, as one of the privileged wealthy, almost everything was a "hobby" to him. Even living. "Like what?"

He stirred his soup. "What my father calls 'creative time-wasting'. Adventure sports, mostly."

She tried to think of something that would fall into that category. "Like skydiving?"

He nodded. "And white-water rafting, and photographic safaris...I was on an archaeological dig in Guatemala last year, and I spent the summer before that cruising the Amazon in a pontoon boat."

Now he was beginning to conform to her idea of a playboy. Exotic places, thrilling adventures... "Sounds dangerous."

"Not really. I always know what I'm doing, and I take along the proper equipment and guides, and..." he glanced meaningfully toward the shuttered window as a gust of wind struck the side of the cabin hard enough to rattle the dishes inside the cupboard. "I make it a point to avoid cold climates."

She shook her head slowly. "You said you had a dull life," she accused. "You said you didn't *do* anything. Stalking tigers and digging for ruins is something."

"Do you think so?"

He seemed so genuinely surprised that she had to laugh. "Don't you?"

"That's not what I meant. Sure, it's something to do, it keeps me in shape, and it has the added advantage of irritating my father... but it's not really doing anything important, is it?"

"Well," she had to admit, "given the broad view, I don't suppose the fate of the world will be irrevocably altered by the way you spend your summer vacations. It's just that, when you said you didn't do *anything*, I pictured you spending the entire day in bed reading the *Times* and eating Godiva chocolates."

Alan chuckled. "I've been known to do that, too."

"So." She bit into a cracker, watching him. "When you're not busy being an explorer and adventurer, what do you do?"

"I'm a professional student."

She blinked. "What?"

"A student. I go to school. I have three master's degrees and I'm working on a doctorate."

"In what?"

"Different things."

"No, I mean the doctorate."

He concentrated on his stew. "Literature. English literature."

"Well." Pam put down her spoon and leaned back. He was becoming more fascinating by the minute. "I'm impressed. You must be really smart."

He shrugged. "Not really. I'm just a good student. I do well on exams, I write brilliant papers, I've aced the system. Learning things is easy for me, but I don't really remember any of them—I guess because I don't have to."

Pam looked at him studiously. "How old are you?"

"Twenty-eight."

"And all those degrees, all the things you've learned—don't you want to do anything with them? All you want to do is go to school?"

He lifted his eyes to her, acknowledging her criticism and the truth of it honestly and without defense. "It's the only thing I've ever been any good at," he said simply.

"You could teach," she pointed out. "You could write, you could—what are your other degrees in?"

"Art history, physical science and graphic design."

She released a small breath of amazement. "Well. Versatile, aren't you?"

He gave another small self-deprecating shrug.

"Anyway, you see," she insisted, "you could do lots of things. Work in a museum, or be a graphic designer, or do whatever it is physical scientists do—"

Alan grinned. "But I don't have to. I'm one of the idle rich, remember?"

She shook her head slowly. "I don't understand why you wouldn't *want* to."

For a moment he looked as though he wanted to say something, then pushed it aside. He lifted his glass in a light salute. "Here's to the Puritan work ethic, something *I've* never understood. Just listening to you talk about it makes me exhausted."

Pam's expression grew serious. "I think you use being rich as an excuse. I think you're afraid to try to do anything useful because you're afraid of the responsibility."

Alan met her gaze evenly and without a hint of censure. "Responsibility is not something they teach in school," he agreed.

His easy acceptance of his own shortcomings was both disconcerting and oddly encouraging. Cautiously, Pam pursued the new line of communication he had opened up between them. "Neither is self-reliance, I'll bet."

He sipped his wine, totally at ease. "If you mean that I could profit from a few months of hard labor and sweat on a Colorado ranch, you're probably right. Is that how you grew up? On a ranch?"

Pam refused to allow his deft attempt to change the subject. "That's not what I meant," she pointed out, "but now that you brought it up, I don't suppose getting up at dawn to take care of the livestock and do my chores every morning before I went to school hurt me any."

He seemed to find that prospect vastly entertaining. "Did you really? Milk the cows and feed the chickens and bale hay?"

Pam frowned a little. Alan made it sound much more bucolic than she liked. Next he would be asking about her 4-H awards. "We didn't have chickens," she replied shortly, "and there are automatic hay-balers these days, you know. But there was plenty to do and we all had to learn how to do it.''

"Do you have a big family?"

"Two brothers and three sisters."

"Older or younger?"

She couldn't imagine that his interest was genuine, but there was nothing in his eyes to suggest that it was not. In fact, he seemed fascinated.

"One younger brother and one younger sister," she answered. "The older ones are married, my younger brother goes to Penn State, and my sister and I live at home."

And then she asked curiously, "Do you always do that—look at people as though there is nothing more important in the world than what they have to say?"

He smiled. "What you have to say *is* important. I want to know about you, that's all."

Though she considered her curiosity about him to be perfectly understandable, being on the receiving end of his interest made Pam distinctly uncomfortable. "I can't imagine why," she said.

"A couple of reasons," Alan replied negligently. "To pass the time, for one thing. For another, as I already pointed out, I like learning things. I'd like to learn about you."

She tried to repress a smile. "You don't have to make me sound like a set of logarithm tables."

A change came over his eyes, but she could not tell whether it was mischief, or something far more serious. "Oh, you don't remind me of logarithms, at all," he said softly. "You remind me of . . . poetry. Or music."

She assumed a studious face. "Classic or modern?"

"Classic," he replied immediately, "with a touch of jazz. Kind of like Yeats as sung by Bob Dylan."

She laughed. The sensation bubbled up inside her, simple pleasure and good feelings, a warmth generated from the spark in his eyes spread over her as if it were a soft comforter, finding its final expression in laughter. It was nice, sitting here with him, talking to him...looking at him. Watching his long fingers curve around the stem of his glass, the muscles of his forearms flex lightly as he lifted it, watching his lips touch the rim . . . watching him smile as he saw her watching him.

"Why don't you have a girlfriend?" she asked again.

She was gratified that this time Alan did not look away, or avoid the subject. His expression grew thoughtful for a moment, as though he were searching for the true answer, but his eyes remained open to her, allowing her the privilege of his thoughts.

"I think," he answered after a moment, "because sleeping with someone isn't enough. I always want more. And I've never met anybody who wants the same things."

"What do you want?" Pam asked, curious.

"Well, then." He gave a smile and lifted his glass. "That's the problem. If I knew that, I'd probably be a lot closer to having it."

"A family?" Pam suggested.

"I've never had a family," he answered simply. "I wouldn't know where to begin."

Pam found that incalculably sad. She had never been without the warmth and support of a large, loving family, and she couldn't imagine life any other way. There had never been any doubt that she would expand that family into the next generation with a home of her own, for that was the way life was meant to be.

"It must be very lonely for you," she said softly.

"Sometimes." Though there was no regret in Alan's voice, there was a yearning in his eyes he could not disguise. And then, with a deliberate effort he erased the expression and said, somewhat more casually, "I guess you and what's-his-name had all sorts of plans for a big family."

Pam swallowed back the stab of hurt his words caused, quickly and forcefully squelching the memories that swirled toward the surface. All day she had avoided thinking about the broken promises, the shattered dreams, the empty future that lay ahead. She would not give in to the weakness now.

"Peter," she said. Her voice was husky and a little shorter than she meant it to be. "His name was Peter."

"Tell me about him."

Pam shot a suspicious glance at Alan, but once again there was nothing in his eyes but simple interest, and even, she thought, a touch of compassion. And there was no reason *not* to talk about Peter. It wasn't as though she bore him any ill will, and what had happened had happened. Sulking about it wouldn't make any difference.

"He was an architect," she said, injecting a note of pride into her voice as she always did when she spoke of Peter. "He was good; brilliant, really. An American firm hired him to build a complex overseas—that's where he's been for the past two years."

"Where he met and swept off her feet the new future Mrs. Peter what's-his-name."

Pam drew a sharp breath, but caught herself just in time. She would not be drawn into an argument with him over something that was none of his business. "He asked me to go with him," she said, after a moment. "But I wanted to teach and—well, I'm not too comfortable away from home, I guess. So I can't blame Peter. I wasn't with him when he needed me...."

"So he went after the first skirt he stumbled over." Alan's voice was dry. "A real prince of a fellow."

"It wasn't like that, at all!" Her previous resolution fled in a surge of temper and her eyes flashed at him. "If you knew Peter you wouldn't say that. He's the most sensitive, compassionate, *gentle* man I've ever known. And strong, too, and generous, and—and brilliant! A man of his talent has special needs, that's all—"

"I see." Alan feigned the dawning of sudden insight. "So talented men—pardon me, strong, compassionate, brilliant, generous, talented men—need more than one woman. One to hold and one *on* hold, so to speak, back in the States."

"You are impossible to talk to! You don't know anything about it and..." She took a deliberate calming breath, adjusting her voice to an almost pleasant tone. ''And I've got better things to do than argue with you about something that isn't even any of your business.''

She stood and took her dishes to the sink, dusting off her hands as she turned. ''I cooked, you do the dishes,'' she informed him. ''If you need me, I'll be back in the Old West with Louis L'Amour.''

Five

I'll give you fifty dollars to put down that book,'' Alan said.

Pam calmly closed the book and held out her hand.

He grinned as he took out his wallet. "If I had known it would be that easy, I would have asked for something bigger."

"There's a limit on what money can buy," Pam replied sweetly. She folded the bill he gave her and tucked it into her jeans pocket, wondering briefly what it would be like to be able to throw away money as though it were a gum wrapper.

"Good thing," Alan murmured dryly, examining the remaining contents of his wallet. "With what I've got left, I probably couldn't buy the time of day."

"You're breaking my heart."

"Twelve dollars and an odd amount of change," he said, tossing his wallet onto the table as he sat down beside her. "That is, at present, the extent of my personal wealth."

He stretched his arm along the back of the sofa and Pam tried not to feel self-conscious as she shifted her legs away from him and sat up a little straighter. "In addition to unlimited worldwide credit," she pointed out.

"Well, as a matter of fact..." For the first time Pam noticed little lines of tension around his eyes, though he kept his voice light—perhaps too light. "My credit's not exactly what it used to be. In fact, you might even say it's nonexistent."

"What do you mean?"

Alan dropped his eyes briefly. He didn't know why he hadn't told her this before; heaven knew he had had ample opportunity. Part of it was the fact that he didn't want to think about it, of course. But the other part was simply that he had enjoyed letting Pamela think he was rich. And it was odd. For most of his life having money had been, at best, something he took for granted; at worst an inconvenience that set him apart from many of his peers at the university. And now all of a sudden it was a very important asset, perhaps the only one he had with which to impress Pamela. He was ashamed both of the deception and the motive behind it.

He looked at her again. "When I stopped for gas yesterday, I discovered my credit cards had been canceled. Naturally, I called the bank, and my accounts were closed, too. It looks as if my father wasn't kidding when he said he was cutting me off."

For a moment she simply stared at him. And then, incredulously, she laughed. "Then you're as poor as I am!"

An absurd relief swept over him. She didn't mind— not that he'd deceived her, not that he wasn't independently wealthy. He wondered if there was anyone else of his acquaintance who would have reacted in the same way, and he couldn't think of a soul.

"Poorer," he reminded her. "You've got fifty dollars."

She chuckled again, and then sobered. "That must've been some fight you had with your dad. What was it about?"

He shrugged uncomfortably. "Basically the same thing we've been arguing about ever since I was twenty-one. He wants me to stop wasting my life and take my rightful place in the company."

"So why don't you?"

"Because I'm *not* twenty-one," he answered shortly, "and I've got a right to do what I want to with my life."

"All right." Pam's face was implacable as she leaned back against the cushions and rested her arm along the back of the sofa. "What *are* you going to do?"

Her arm was crooked at the elbow and her fingers dangled within six inches of his. She had short fingers with neatly trimmed, unpolished nails, and her hands were the same creamy color as her face. That surprised him, for he would have expected the hands of an outdoor person like her to be tanned and a little rough, not soft and sweet and . . . sexy. He had never thought of a woman's hands as being sexy before.

He glanced back up at her. "I haven't thought about it."

Pam's gaze was steady and unrelenting. It was like looking into the face of his conscience. "Now might be a good time," she suggested.

Alan sighed heavily and leaned his head back against the sofa. "That's why I hate being stuck in this place. Too much time to think and too much I don't want to think about. If I could just keep moving things would work themselves out."

"If you kept moving, you'd run out of gas," Pam pointed out practically.

That made him smile. "So you're telling me that being trapped in a blizzard in the middle of nowhere is the best thing that could have happened to me." And he was thinking, *Maybe it is*. Sitting here with her, looking into a face that was both gentle and stern, lovely and uncomplicated, watching the changing expressions in her eyes and wondering what emotion they might reflect next, he couldn't think of any other place he'd rather be.

"At least you have time to make a plan."

"I never make plans. It takes all the spontaneity out of life." He looked at her hand again, so near to his. All he had to do was stretch out his fingers and they would touch hers, open his hand and close it about hers. He wondered if her skin was as soft as it looked.

He was so busy wondering that he didn't notice how inappropriately flippant his last words had sounded, nor did he notice the slight chill that had come into Pam's eyes. But her tone was edged with disgust and frustration as she said, "You're not worried at all, are you?"

Maybe it was her words, maybe it was the way she said them. Alan felt the protective barrier he had built around his deepest emotions begin to buckle, and desperately he tried to shore it up. "Worried? Of course, I'm worried. If I weren't worried sick, I would have been putting some heavy moves on you before now, you can bet on that. I'm so worried I don't even know a good thing when I see it, that's how bad it is."

But his attempt at levity fell short. She looked at him with the patient inevitability of one who had never run away from a problem in her life, and the last of his defenses crumbled.

He stood up abruptly, pushing back his hair in a short, tense gesture as he walked away from her. "I'm worried, okay? Not because of the money, or the police, but because I hate fighting with him. And it seems like I've been fighting with him all my life."

Pam didn't know what to say. Briefly she remembered their agreement not to invade one another's privacy with prying questions. But hadn't he already broken that contract when he started badgering her about Peter? Besides, it simply wasn't her nature to stand by and watch someone wrestle with a problem when it was possible she could do something to help.

After a moment she ventured, "Maybe you should look at it from his point of view. After all, he worked hard for what he has and—"

"He didn't work hard." Alan thrust his hands into his pockets and she could see his fingers tighten into angry fists. The movement brought the material of his pants taut across his buttocks, and his shoulders were squared with tension. "He inherited a steel and coal-mining empire and turned it into a megalithic monster that rapes the land and gobbles up decent, hard-working people like hors d'oeuvres, and I don't *want* that. In the past three years he's been investigated five times by the EPA. Last year he closed down a plant that put a whole town out of work. Maybe he's not a bad man, maybe he didn't have any alternatives—I'm not passing judgment on something I don't know anything about. But it's a bad business, and I don't want to be involved."

Pam hesitated. "Did you ever tell him that?"

He shook his head slowly. "I tried. We don't communicate too well." He turned then, and there was a distant, vaguely sardonic smile on his lips. "This is going to sound like one of those poor-little-rich-boy stories, but when I was fifteen I came to spend the summer with my dad. He was involved in some sort of antitrust suit at the time and was spending most of his time in court. When I got to the house he wasn't home, so I went down to the courthouse to surprise him. He was just coming out of the building, with a mob of reporters and lawyers all around him, every-body talking at once, and he didn't notice me. So, as kind of a joke, I held the car door open for him, waiting for him to recognize me. You know what he did? He tipped me. He never even knew I was there.''

The humor faded completely from his face as he finished, ''I got a cab to the airport and went back to school. A few days later, he remembered I was supposed to be with him that summer and called to find out what had happened. I told him I had a chance to go to Switzerland with my roommate's family and he sounded relieved to have me off his hands. But I didn't go to Switzerland. I stayed in the dorm all summer, with a few of the other boys who didn't have any place to go.''

He looked at her, and what Pam noticed about that quiet gaze was that there was no bitterness within it, nor resentment. Just simple honesty. ''Now he wants his only son to follow in his footsteps,'' Alan said, ''and I've spent most of my life trying to avoid doing just that. I don't want anyone to ever remember me the way I remember him. And if that makes me a bad son or a worthless person, then I guess that's what I am.''

A great many things were going through Pam's mind, and she couldn't put any of them into words. What a complex man Alan Donovan was, and how shallowly she had judged him. She kept thinking about her own father, big and outspoken and interminably cheerful; when he was stern his face could reform an unruly child with a look, but he had a heart as soft as melted wax. Her childhood memories were a cacophony of noisy mealtimes, sibling arguments that were as fiery as they were short-lived, and lots and lots of laughter. When she tried to think of growing up alone, she couldn't even imagine the emptiness.

Alan's background, his experiences, were so far removed from hers that the two of them might well have originated on separate planets. And yet, as different as they were, she felt a bond there, as though his sharing had made her a part of what he was. She didn't understand, and couldn't pretend to, the things that had made him into the man he was today. But she wanted to understand, and most importantly, she felt his pain.

She got up from the sofa and slowly, hesitantly, she slipped her arm through his. He looked surprised at the gesture, but to Pam it felt right. "I don't think you're worthless," she said softly.

At that moment Alan didn't feel worthless, either. Her touch flowed over him as if it were a benediction, simple, sweet, and unencumbered by the complexities and uncertainties that had haunted him all his life. He thought suddenly how good it would be if every moment could be as pure and as unclouded as this one.

He smiled. "You're a good listener."

Without even thinking about it, Pam let her hand slide down his arm, entwining her fingers with his. "It's easier to talk about someone else's problems than your own."

Her fingers were as soft as he had imagined, a honey-eyed touch that infused his veins with a drowsy kind of contentment. She smelled like almonds and honey, and he thought he could go on forever like this, just standing there holding her hand.

"Sometimes I think that's what we're all about," he said. "I mean, why there's more than one person on earth. So we can listen to each other's problems."

His returned handclasp was secure and gentle, somehow sealing a new bond of intimacy between them that registered in a glow that started in the pit of Pam's stomach and spread like a delicate yellow light through her limbs, warming her wherever it touched. She could feel the faint scratchy texture of his wool sweater against her wrist, and the subtle heat of his body against her arm. For the first time since the accident she stopped worrying about the snow and the wind and the possibility of rescue. And Peter.

She said, "I guess maybe talking, and listening, makes us realize our problems aren't so bad after all."

His smile deepened, forming faint radiant lines at the edges of his eyes. "Darlin'," he said, "with world hunger, earthquakes, floods, fires, planes falling out of the sky every day and nuclear holocaust looming on the horizon—we don't have any problems, at all."

She laughed a little, squeezing his fingers. "That's what I like. A man who can put things into perspective."

The slow, gentle light that filled his eyes held her captive, drawing her close in a way that no simple embrace could have done. Contentment bloomed within her, low and subtle, and she thought, *I like you, Alan Donovan. I like you more than anyone I've met in a long time, more than I ever thought I would; more, even, than I ever liked Peter...* The realization shocked and confused her and she felt color sting her cheeks. Quickly she dropped her eyes and pulled her hand away from his.

She dug into her pocket and produced the bill he had given her. "Under the circumstances," she said, "I think I'd better return this." When he started to protest she lifted a hand. "I took it under false pretenses," she explained. "I'd finished the book, anyway."

He grinned and took the bill from her. "We'll leave it for McMurty," he said, dropping it onto a table by the window.

"Fair enough." She gave him a quick smile and started to turn away before that soft light in his eyes could capture her again and begin to stir up more compelling emotions she did not want to examine.

But he caught both her hands this time, startling her into a tingling awareness of his fingers on hers, strong and gentle, sending trails of warmth along her nerve paths and through her pulses. She did not know what she would find in his face when she turned, but the solemnity of his gaze surprised her.

"Pamela," he said, and dropped his eyes briefly. When he looked at her again it was with the kind of openness and sincerity she had learned to associate with him, but beneath it all there was a struggle, and she knew this was difficult for him to say. "I just wanted you to know...I've always intended to get my life straightened out. I just never had a good enough reason for doing it before. What you said earlier, about my using being rich as an excuse—you were right, but there's more to it than that. Sometimes, when people don't expect anything of you, the easiest thing in the world is to live up to their expectations."

"You don't have to explain to me, Alan," she said softly. But she was glad, so glad, that he had.

"I want to." His fingers tightened on hers. "What you think is important to me."

A glow filled Pam that started from the touch of his fingers and found its final release in a hesitant, almost wondering smile. "That's funny," she said, almost to herself. "I can't remember my opinion ever being really important to anyone before."

His expression changed, becoming curious, and she knew he was wondering about Peter. Before he could speak, she said quickly, "The wood bin is getting low. I'd better go get some more."

He took the hint, to her great relief. But she was sorry when he released her hands. "I'll do it."

"No, that's okay." A few minutes alone in the icy wind was exactly what she needed to restore her equilibrium. "It's no trouble, and you don't have a coat—"

"I found a big lumberjack coat in the closet," he said, starting toward it, "and a pair of boots. We'll both go. It'll be faster that way."

A moment later Pam was glad for his company. The thickness of the cabin walls had disguised the increasing ferocity of the storm, and when she opened the back door, Pam was shocked at what she found. Snow was coming down in thick, icy pellets, and visibility was little more than the length of her outstretched arm. The wind whipped around the side of the building, then doubled back on itself, forming a continuous fog of ice vapor and lashing snow. Pam felt a horrible despair congeal and settle in the pit of her stomach. She had thought that they had passed through the worst of the storm on that hideous trek up here. How could it be getting worse? How *could* it?

As Alan pulled the door closed behind them she turned and gestured the way toward the woodshed. Trying to speak was pointless in the wind. Alan, fumbling to pull on a pair of gloves he had found in the pocket of the coat, nodded assent and flipped the collar up over his ears, hunching his shoulders against the cold. Pam didn't wait for him, but led the way to the shed, some fifty feet distant.

The short walk was almost as strenuous as the hike to the cabin had been. They fought the wind and the stinging snow with every step, and snow drifted up to Pam's calves in some places. When they reached the relative shelter of the shed, both of them took a moment to rest out of the wind, breathing hard.

"Why," Alan demanded after a moment, struggling for an even breath, "does he keep his wood—so far from the house?"

"T-t-termites." That single word was all the breath she could spare for an explanation, and she bent to start filling her arms with wood.

Snow had dusted the tops of the logs closest to the entrance, and, following Pam's example, Alan filled his arms with wood from the back. Hoping to avoid another trip, they each took as much as they could possibly carry, and shared a look of abject dread before stepping out into the storm again.

The heavy load of wood made the trip back even more difficult than the trip out had been. Pam's blood roared in her ears from exertion and her legs shuffled along as though bound by heavy chains. Already the wind had blown away their footprints, and though Pam tried to keep a straight course to avoid stepping in a drift, that task, too, was almost impossible. When she saw the shadow of the back porch come into view she determinedly increased her pace—and her legs sank knee-deep into snow. She flailed a moment for balance, but the load of wood pulled her over and she sprawled face-downward in the snow.

For a moment she was too stunned to react, then she felt Alan's arms around her, pulling her to her feet. His cheek was pressed to hers as he shouted, "Are you all right?"

She nodded, gasping and clinging to his arms for balance as she struggled to right herself. A stab of wind slashed through her clothing and what she really wanted to do was wrap herself in his arms, drawing close to his protection and warmth as they hurried toward the shelter of the cabin; she forced herself to push away and turn to gather up the wood she had dropped.

"Leave it!" Alan caught her arm, trying to pull her back. "I'll come back for it later!"

"No!" Later—even five minutes later—the wood they had struggled so hard to get this far would be covered by snow, and they would have to endure the agonizing journey back to the woodshed again. But Pam couldn't waste energy explaining that to him. She tore her arm away and quickly began to gather up her wood, leaving him no choice but to do the same.

The warmth of the cabin brought a rush of stinging circulation back to Pam's limbs as Alan kicked the door closed behind them. She stumbled to the stove and let her wood drop with a thunderous clatter, blinking back tears of pain and frustration. "It's all wet!" she cried angrily.

Alan dumped his wood beside hers with only slightly more care. "You are the most stubborn woman I've ever met! Next time I'll do it, okay? It'll be easier than picking you up out of the snow and fighting over a few sticks of wood—"

"You couldn't even find your way to the shed without me!" She turned on him furiously. "And those *sticks* are all that's standing between life and death for us, or are you too blind to see that? This isn't a *game*, do you understand? It's not a rich kid's adventure or a pretend survival exercise and nobody's waiting outside to lend a hand in case we get in trouble—we *are* in trouble, real trouble, and I'm doing the best I can!"

He paused in the process of tugging off his gloves and looked at her for a long time. Her eyes were snapping and her fists were clenched and her chest rose and fell rapidly. His expression was unreadable.

Then he said quietly, "I know. I'm scared, too."

Suddenly she was in his arms. His embrace was tight and secure and she clung to him, burying her face in the wool jacket and trying not to cry. "Oh, Alan," she said miserably at last. "I'm sorry."

She could feel the smile in his voice as his cheek rested against her hair. "That's okay. At least it got your circulation going."

She managed a rueful smile. Even though he couldn't see, it made her feel better. "Not for yelling at you. I'm sorry for that, too, but—for bringing you here." Her voice caught there and she let her arms drop from his shoulders to his waist, tightening them. She pressed her forehead against his chest, her eyes lowered and her voice muffled. "I thought the storm would blow itself out, I swear I did, I thought we could wait it out and then go for help—but you were right, if we had stayed with the cars someone would have found us by now. Now the storm is getting worse and no one knows where we are and it's all my fault—"

"Hey." He took her shoulders and pushed her away a little. "That's enough of that. If we had stayed with the cars we might both be frozen by now, you know that as well as I do. I'm lucky you came along and we're both lucky you knew where this place was, so let's not hear any more about what might have been. You're not acting very heroic, you know that?"

That drew a weak smile from her, and she let her face rest against his chest again. His arms came around her naturally, comfortingly. "I don't feel very heroic."

"Well, that's okay, too, I guess, as long as you don't feel sad—and stop trying to blame yourself for something that can't possibly be your fault."

His wool jacket was scratchy and damp with melting snow, smelling faintly of wood smoke and mustiness. But beneath its texture she could feel the shape of his arms and the strength of his chest, and it was a good, safe feeling to be held against him. She murmured, "So you're not sorry you let me drag you up here?"

"Sorry?" He dipped his head, coaxing her to look at him. "Don't you know meeting you was the best thing that ever happened to me?"

Their faces were not even an inch apart. Pam could see the flecks of gold that tipped his lashes, they were that close. And as he looked at her the teasing smile in his eyes slowly faded into something deeper, and Pamela forgot to breathe. He repeated softly, with something like a touch of wonder, "The very best thing . . ." And he kissed her.

His lips touched hers lightly at first, so lightly that she thought he would pull away. She couldn't have stopped him if he had, for everything within her was suspended, helpless with uncertainty and anticipation. She didn't know, in that first surprised moment, what she wanted or expected, whether this was right or wrong, whether she should push away or hold him closer; half of her was crying out for him to stop and the other half would have cried if he had stopped.

There was a moment of sweet hesitation and his lips almost left hers. Pam drew in a breath, though whether it was of protest or plea she could not be sure. She caught a brief glimpse of his eyes, hazy and lit by a glow she didn't completely understand. Then his hands dropped to her waist, drawing her close; he moved his head slightly and his mouth covered hers.

A rush of heat welled up inside Pam and left her dizzy. Her limbs were like wax, melting into his embrace, and bright spots of color danced behind her closed lids. She hadn't realized how hungry she was for a loving touch, how helpless she was against the power of a kiss, how eager to surrender to the passion that could flower between a man and a woman.... No, not just any man. Alan. For no one had made her feel like this before.

His kiss consumed every part of her. Nerve endings tingled and sparked with awareness; cell fibers flared to life and expanded to receive him. She felt the warmth of his face spreading to her skin, his fingers pressing into her back, his thighs taut against hers. He tasted of wine and heat and his fresh forest scent enveloped her. Her greedy senses drank him in like a potent drug and the heady pleasure filled her, leaving her wanting more.

She moved her hands to his neck, wanting to feel the texture of his skin and the silky strands of his hair, but her gloves were in the way. Too many layers of clothes stood between them; bulky coats and scarves that kept skin from touching skin and muted the sensation of bodies straining to press close. But even that frustration, in its own way, increased the pleasure, focusing her attention on the parts of him she could touch and sharpening the anticipation of need. For that endless moment wanting and having were almost the same, and the simple joy of it was enough.

They separated slowly, tasting and touching and parting with exquisite reluctance and care. Yet even when the kiss was ended it lingered, in the blending of their breaths, the shared flush of passion that heated their faces, and in their eyes, which reflected a glow of wonder and the image of each other.

Pam felt giddy, disoriented, shaken and uncertain...but delighted. The radiance of pleasure had her in its thrall and though she knew she should be careful, she should be hesitant and sensible, she didn't want the moment to end. She said huskily, "That was nice."

The light in his eyes flared and faded as he searched her face. "Yes," he agreed softly. "It was."

His lips were still moist from the contact with hers. She wanted to touch those lips, to trace their contours with her fingers and explore the softness and the warmth, but she didn't want to move her hands long enough to take off her gloves. She didn't want to move, at all. She wanted to stand like this in the circle of his embrace and the glow of thoughtless contentment forever. She smiled into his eyes. "Do you want to do it again?"

He answered softly, "I want to do more than that."

Her heart, which had only just begun to regain its normal rhythm, caught in a breath and accelerated helplessly. She looked at him and she thought, *So do I.* And that was when the sweet-spun spell of careless pleasure began to crack, and slowly shatter into the sharp edges of reality.

It was true. She wanted to make love to this man she had known less than five hours and would never see again. Another moment and she would have abandoned herself to him entirely, intent on nothing but the pleasure they could share. That was not her.

Pamela Mercer was simple, straightforward, responsible; a solid citizen with small dreams and modest ambitions. She followed the rules, she paid her dues, and she spent her days in ordinary ways with ordinary people, doing the expected thing. And with all that going for her, she had still managed to make a mess of romance and lose her fiancé to another woman. Did she think that going to bed with a stranger could fix *that*?

No, one foolish mistake could not counteract another, and wild, passionate encounters had no place in her life—no more than did men like Alan Donovan. To him it would be a sweet memory that would soon fade in the wake of other conquests, other adventures. But she would be left feeling only empty and sad and more of a failure than ever.

Pam dropped her eyes, and Alan knew as surely as if she had spoken the words, what she was thinking. An urgency tightened his muscles as he felt the magical moment slipping away and everything within him demanded that he stop it. It would be so easy. A touch on her face, a kiss, a slow, sweet surrender. He could make love to her, and it would be wonderful. He wanted to make love to her with all his soul.

"But I won't," he said quietly. There was a hoarse texture to his voice that startled him almost as much as the words had done. He hadn't intended to say that. He didn't *want* to say that.

He touched her face, lifting her chin. Her eyes were wide and confused, wanting and reluctant. "I told you before," he said, with difficulty, "that it's important what you think of me. I want to make love with you

right now more than I've ever wanted anything before. But I want it to be for the right reasons. I don't
want you to think I'm using you. And..." He took a
breath. "I don't want to be used, either."

She was startled. "But I—"

His lips quirked with a resigned kind of smile and
he made a brief gesture with his wrist. "Isn't that what
this is all about? The Great Escape?" Even as he spoke
he couldn't believe he was saying this. He couldn't
believe that, for the first time in his life, he was seeing
the broader picture, putting someone else's needs before his own—being responsible. He didn't want to do
this. But deep down inside he knew that he wanted
something else even more, and that something was so
fragile, so delicate, he dared not even recognize what
it was yet. He only knew that it had to be protected.

"We're both running from something," he told her
gently, "and it would be easy to use each other to hide
behind. I've...done that too often, in the past. I don't
want it to be that way with you. And I don't think you
want it, either."

Pam slowly lowered her eyes, and the emotion that
filled her was so strange, so new and unexpected, that
she couldn't even define it, much less understand it.
She only knew that it felt good. Warm and secure
and...good.

She looked up at him, and smiled tentatively.
"You're quite a guy," she said.

He made a rueful face. "So I'm constantly told."
He leaned forward and kissed her lightly on the forehead. "Now," he said briskly, "let's see about building up that fire."

But as they knelt to gather up the wood he reached out and touched her cheek with a gloved hand. There was a trace of uncertainty in his eyes. "Friends?"

Pam smiled. Again that wonderful contentment stirred within her, and she had never felt so purely happy in her life. "Friends," she said.

Six

So I followed her for four blocks, right? I mean, I was like one of those crazed characters in a perfume commercial, dodging traffic, jaywalking, leaping over trashcans . . . and all the while I was planning these incredibly witty opening lines. I'm talking sheer poetry here. If I had written down half the things I thought of to win this lady's heart, I could have had a best-seller.''

Alan smiled in self-indulgent reminiscence and Pam, delighted with the tale, smiled back. "So?" she prompted. "What happened?"

"Well, I finally caught up with her at the corner of Fifth Avenue, and there she was—a combination of

Christie Brinkley and Ingrid Bergman, the most gorgeous creature I'd ever seen in my life. And there I was, sixteen years old, dumbstruck in love with this woman I'd never seen before she got out of a cab on Park Avenue. I screwed up my courage and tapped her on the arm, and she turned around to look at me—and all I could think of to say was, 'You're beautiful.' Well, she looked at me for a minute, and then she said 'I know.' And then the light changed, and she crossed the street. I must have stood there for ten minutes, wondering what had happened.''

Pam chuckled, and Alan added, ''I learned two very important things about myself that day. First, I don't make a very good first impression. And second, beautiful women aren't my type.''

Pam's eyes danced as she sipped her wine. ''I think you learned something else—that you might be just the least bit impulsive when it comes to romance.''

''Ah,'' responded Alan with a lift of his finger, ''but I'm loyal. That was twelve years ago, and I've never completely gotten over her.''

Pam laughed again, enjoying the mischievous light that played in his eyes and the way the lamplight gleamed on the golden hairs of his forearm when he lifted his wineglass in salute. They were sitting on the sofa, drinking the last of the bottle of wine they had opened at lunch, or at least Alan was sitting. Pam was half reclining against the cushions, her legs stretched across Alan's lap and her feet propped up on the other side of him. Alan's hand rested comfortably on her knee, and it was a testament to the new and relaxed intimacy that had developed between them that this position did not feel suggestive, or threatening in any way. It was simply easy and natural.

"Now your turn," Alan said. "Tell me a secret."

"I don't have any secrets. No good ones, anyway." And she looked at him curiously. "What is your type?"

"Of what?"

"Woman."

"The type that doesn't say goodbye," he answered without hesitation. And at her questioning expression he added, "Or at least the type who would have the common courtesy to miss me a little after I'm gone." He frowned a little, trying to explain, "It all seems so—cavalier with the women I've known. Easy come, easy go. I'd like to think that the woman I've given my heart to at least sheds a few tears when it's over."

"Maybe you give your heart too easily," Pam suggested.

His expression softened, and there was too much meaning behind his gentle, direct gaze. "Maybe I do."

There was a slight tightness in Pam's throat which she did her best to eliminate with a quick sip of wine. "So," she demanded brightly, "do you shed any tears when they're gone?"

He grinned. "No. Most of the time I'm relieved."

She chuckled. "You reap what you sow."

But Pam suspected his last remark was more of a teasing attempt to live up to her playboy image of him than a statement of fact. Though he might have many foibles and peculiarities of which she was yet unaware, he wasn't the kind of man to take relationships casually. That much she had known about him from the beginning.

Their shared smiles faded into a comfortable silence, and for a time there was nothing but the creak and rattle of the wind through the trees outside and the muted roar of burning logs inside the stove. Neither felt pressed to talk, and even Alan seemed to have burned off the hyperkinetic energy he had displayed when they first arrived. Pam thought about how strange it was, that so much could change in such a short time.

When she had first met Alan she had thought him shallow, self-involved and not particularly bright. He was an oddity, a touch of glamour in an out-of-the-way place, and he intrigued her the way tabloid headlines intrigued her when she was standing in line at the supermarket. But over the hours, almost minute by minute, he had grown in dimension for her until he now bore very little resemblance at all to the man she had first met.

She had discovered him to be sensitive and thoughtful and painstakingly honest, with a quirky sense of humor that matched her own. The complexity of his needs made her own life seem rich by comparison, but he faced them bravely and wasn't afraid to reveal his weaknesses and uncertainties. She couldn't remember ever knowing anyone who shared so easily and so completely. He no longer reminded her of a tabloid headline at all, and in fact it seemed as if she had known him for years.

Sitting there with him in cozy silence, it was too easy to let her mind drift. The memory of his kiss was a real and living thing which she kept at bay only with great effort, and when she relaxed her guard the sensations came flooding back as clearly as if it had happened only a moment ago...as if it were happening now. And she couldn't stop herself from taking it further. How effortlessly her imagination supplied the details—his touch upon her flesh, their limbs entwined in passion, lying in one another's arms afterward, just holding one another.... And beyond the lovemaking, there was a hazy vision of days just like this, sitting by the fire, talking and laughing, and nights of warm rapture she couldn't even imagine. Together, just like this, secure and content with one another, forever.

The ease with which the daydream was conjured surprised her, but she knew that was just what it was— a daydream. Everyone was entitled to those once in a while. Alan was right: being snowbound up here, out of touch with reality and trying to forget too many things—not the least of which was how scared they really were—was a hazardous emotional setup.

Neither of them could trust such impulses or feelings, because it was simply too easy to forget that the world went on beyond this snowy mountaintop and when they returned to it each would go his separate way. She had just made one mistake with Peter—a drastic, foolish, life-altering mistake—and she had no intention of compounding things by stumbling directly into the arms of the first man who crossed her path. She wouldn't be so stupid. There would be no endless days together by the fire nor heated nights of shared passion; Pam knew that very well. The challenge lay in remembering it.

Alan's fingers traced an absent pattern on the inside seam of her jeans, over her knee. It was an innocent movement, delicate and harmless, and he did not even appear to be aware that he was doing it. But Pam was very aware. A tight trail of sensation traveled from the touch of his fingers up the inside of her thigh and beyond, making her skin prickle and her muscles contract. And then, as though suddenly catching himself in error, Alan stopped and looked at her and gave a small apologetic smile.

"How about a game of Scrabble?" he suggested.

Pam shook her head, scolding herself for her thoughts of a moment ago and trying to relax. "No, thanks. I'd have to be crazy to play Scrabble with an English major."

"Okay. I've got another game." Alan leaned back against the sofa and removed his hand casually—he hoped—from her knee, cupping both hands around his glass. "It's a sort of getting-to-know-you game; people play it at parties. I name one thing I like, you name two things, I name three and so on."

"Sounds like a stupid game to me."

"It's more fun with a group, but it's guaranteed to take your mind off snowy afternoons. I'll start. I like..." He thought a moment. "Fast cars."

"I like station wagons."

"One more."

"Onion soup."

"No, no, you're supposed to stay in category. Fast cars, bicycles, dogsleds—modes of transportation."

"I don't like anything else that moves. Onion soup," she insisted.

He groaned. "Why did it have to be food? We're sitting here with a cabinet full of canned spaghetti and all you want to talk about is food? All right," he lifted a defensive hand as she started to protest. "The category is food. I like Belgian chocolate and strawberries with fresh cream and . . ." He closed his eyes in brief sensual reminiscence. "White-chocolate eclairs."

"Cinnamon toast," responded Pam, beginning to fall into the spirit of the game. "Roasted marshmallows, my mom's lemon cake, and bacon when it's cooking on a cold morning."

"Hot chocolate, mulled cider with cinnamon sticks . . ."

"Those aren't foods," she pointed out.

"You changed the category with bacon to things that smell good. That's how the game is played, by association." He continued, "I like cocoa-butter tanning oil, honey-and-almond shampoo and . . ." he looked at her. "You."

Pam's cheeks warmed. "How did you know what kind of shampoo I used?"

"It smells good."

She made herself break his smiling gaze, and she sipped her wine. "I think this is a silly game."

"You're probably right." With a light pressure on her knees, Alan moved her legs aside and stood up. He didn't want to, but her nearness was beginning to act far too strongly on him. He couldn't even talk about her hair without wondering what it would look like out of its braid and cascading around her shoulders, how it would feel, gathered in the palms of his hands and brushing against his naked skin. Her most innocent smile could send his mind chasing down outrageously erotic paths, and even the sound of her voice was like a gentle caress against his most sensual nerve centers.

This was all a new experience for Alan. He was unused to wanting anything strongly, and women were of such easy availability in his life that desire had, over the years, lost its edge. He considered himself jaded, sophisticated and wise in the ways of love, a man whose passions were carefully under control. But he had only to look at Pamela to become aroused, and the physical yearning was only half of it. He *wanted* her; he wanted to know her and touch her, to understand her thoughts and share her feelings and memorize her experiences as if they were his own. He wanted to make her smile and he wanted her to lean on him when she was sad; everything about her excited him, made him curious and left him longing for more—so he made up silly games to hear the sound of her voice and he told her he would be her friend so that he could be close to her, and he pretended that nothing unusual was happening inside him, at all.

He walked over to the window, where he had discovered a chink in one of the shutters that provided a five-degree view of the world outside. His hand clenched unconsciously on the wineglass. God, would the snow never stop? If only it would let up, just for an hour or so, someone might see the smoke from the chimney and come to investigate. But the snow slashed against the windows with unrelenting ferocity, branches overhead sighed and moaned, and it was becoming indisputably clear that they were going to have to spend the night here.

His voice sounded laudably casual as he announced, "It's getting dark."

Pam glanced at her watch. "I guess so. It's almost five o'clock."

Alan cleared his throat and glanced toward the bed. "I don't suppose there's any chance we could be mature about the sleeping arrangements?"

Pam got up to put another log on the fire, sparing him a wary look. "In what way?"

"Well, there's only one bed and two of us, but we're both adults, perfectly capable of controlling our—"

"No." She caught the edge of a repressed smile as she opened the stove door and bent to lay on another log. "No, we can't be mature about the sleeping arrangements. I'll take the sofa."

"You don't have to do that," he protested.

She flashed him a rather impish grin. "Oh, yes I do. It's warmer here, in front of the fire. You can have the bed and be as mature as you want."

Alan turned one palm upward in a gesture of resignation, a sheepish grin tugging at his own lips. "I *am* trying to be noble about this thing."

She looked up at him, her face flushed and golden with the heat of the stove, and she answered in a subdued tone, "So am I."

Alan came over to her slowly, but he didn't touch her. He leaned against the back of the sofa, his feet planted firmly apart and his shoulders relaxed, regarding her soberly as she made a last few adjustments to the fire with the poker. "Can you explain to me," he said simply, "why we're going to so much

trouble to deny ourselves something we both obviously want?''

Pam closed the door and locked it, taking her time
before she turned around. Her face still held the heat
of the fire, but her hands were clasped tightly before
her and there was distress in her eyes. ''Just because
you want something, Alan,'' she answered carefully,
''doesn't mean you can have it—or even that it would
be good for you if you did.''

More than anything at that moment Alan wanted to
take her into her arms, to ease away that closed, tight
look from her face and to make her believe—to
somehow make her believe—that *he* would be good
for her. But he couldn't even make himself believe
that.

After a moment he managed a smile, and a light
shrug. ''I was just curious. I'm new at this self-
sacrificing business.''

She seemed to relax a little. ''Keep practicing. It
builds character.''

He lifted his glass. ''Well, I can always use more of
that.''

Pam wiped her dusty hands on her jeans pockets
and glanced at him shyly. ''Actually,'' she observed,
''I think you have more character than you realize.''

And then, before he could question that odd remark, her expression grew worried and she inquired,
''Alan, what are you going to do?''

He had no trouble at all following the drift of her
conversation. Though he had diligently tried to avoid
it, that question hadn't been far from his own mind in
the past hour or so. But the surprising thing was that,

having brought the entire situation out into the open for Pamela seemed to have defused it. He was no longer angry when he thought about his father, he no longer wrestled with frustration and impotence. For the first time he was able to look at the situation calmly and with a measure of control, even detachment. Knowing Pamela, and sharing with her, had put everything into perspective.

He glanced thoughtfully into his wineglass, then back at her. "I can tell you what's going to happen," he said after a moment. "When my dad thinks I've suffered enough, he'll send me a check, quietly reinstate my credit and everything will go back to normal. He doesn't have enough..." he grimaced a little... "*character* to stick by a decision for very long." He shrugged with a semblance of his old nonchalance. "If I were smart, I'd just lay low until then."

She asked carefully, "Is that what you want? For everything to be back to normal?"

Alan couldn't answer right away. Yesterday the answer would have been an unqualified "Yes." Yesterday words such as "character" and "responsibility" had meant nothing to him, and all he wanted was to live his life the way he had chosen with no hassles. Now it suddenly wasn't so simple any more.

"I don't like conflict," he answered after a moment, doing his best to be honest—with her, and with himself. "And I'm not very good with challenges. I've got three months' work left on my doctorate and I guess the one thing I can be proud of myself for is that I always finish what I start. And there's no way I can finish without money."

He took a breath, and met her eyes bravely. "No,"
he admitted, "I don't want things to go back to normal. I always thought, I guess, in the back of my
mind, that I was punishing my father with my life-
style, but what I was really doing was building a trap
for myself. I don't want that to go on for the rest of my
life. I want..." And there he had to stop, because
suddenly his mind was flooded with visions of things
he wanted, things he had never guessed at before,
things that were so rich and vast he could not even begin to put them into words. Things that had to do with
dignity and purpose and the meaning of life. A place
to call home, and someone to welcome him there. A
sense of belonging, a reason to be. The feeling he had
when he was with Pamela.

He blinked against the sudden confusion and tried
to smile. He did not entirely succeed. "I guess," he
finished lightly, "I want what you have. Character."

Her laugh sounded a little forced. "You're the first
person who's ever said *that*." Then, with a deft change
of subject, she turned toward the kitchen. "Are you
hungry?"

"I suppose."

He followed her, a slight frown hovering about his
eyes as he watched her quick, deliberately energetic
movements. It disturbed him to hear her put herself
down like that; it wasn't right and it didn't suit her. He
wanted to get to know her, to understand what was
going on in her mind and to comfort her, if he could,
the way her mere presence comforted him.

But she had erected a barrier between them, subtle
but unmistakable, and he didn't know any way around

it. All he could do was approach her directly, as he had done from the beginning.

He drained the last of his wine and put the glass in the sink. "Pamela, will you tell me something?"

She opened the cabinet and looked inside. "If I can."

He lifted himself to the countertop beside the sink, out of her way, and kept his tone casual. "A little while ago, you said that your opinion had never been important to anyone before. What did you mean?"

She shrugged, pushing aside a couple of cans to get to the back of the cabinet. "Oh, you know. The middle child in a family always gets crowded out. Here's some hamburger helper, but no hamburger. What I wouldn't give for a nice juicy steak."

"Is that all?" Alan inquired. "Just being the middle child?"

"Oh, I don't know." She selected a can of chili, looked at it skeptically and returned it. "I'm twenty-five years old, I still live at home, the most important contribution I make to society is teaching kids how to tie their shoelaces. You can't really say I strike a very imposing figure, now can you?"

"I disagree," Alan countered with a grin. "If it weren't for people like you, we'd have an awful lot of grown-ups tripping over their shoelaces. That could be embarrassing at a board meeting, not to mention a presidential summit."

That made her smile, although Alan detected a trace of wistfulness in it. She moved around some more cans, not looking at him, and he said seriously, "I don't understand why you say you're not important.

You're one of the smartest, most together women I've ever met. You—"

"Why?" she interrupted him with a short, derisive sound. "Because I know how to light an oil lamp and start a generator?"

"Well, yes—"

"That's no big deal." She dismissed him with a turn of her wrist. "Not around here, anyway."

"It's a very big deal to me."

"So you're easily impressed." A well-disguised note of tension crept into her voice as she closed one cabinet door and opened another. "But even you have to admit there's nothing particularly special about me. I mean, I've never jumped out of an airplane or cruised the Amazon or been to Europe. I didn't even finish college, for heaven's sake. About the only significant thing I've ever done was get engaged to an important man, and I couldn't even make that work."

Alan bit back a swift retort, confused. Was this about him or about Peter? And what could either of them have done to make a woman like Pam feel insignificant? He kept his tone even as he commented, "That's funny. You're apologizing for not finishing college and I always feel like I have to apologize for making it a career."

"I wasn't apologizing." Her voice was a little sharp. "I was just stating a fact."

"So why didn't you finish?"

"It just seemed like a waste of time, and I didn't need a degree when I started teaching preschool."

"Don't you like what you do?"

"Oh, yes." She turned then, and the glow in her eyes was unmistakable. "Yes, I really do. I love the kids, and I love watching them grow and change and actually *learn* from me, you know? I like planning lessons and making bulletin boards and..." She laughed a little. "I even like the smell of that awful wheat paste. But..." The glow in her eyes began to fade. "It's like Peter always said, it's not as though I'm irreplaceable or anything. It doesn't take any special skills to fill my place, and I don't know, maybe I love it too much. If I had gone with Peter when he asked me, instead of staying here because I didn't want to leave the kids..."

Alan saw the shadow of pain cross her face, and his muscles clenched against it. Pam gave a sad little smile and a shrug of her shoulder that tugged at his heart. "I guess I just wanted to hang on as long as I could. It was selfish of me, but I knew I'd have to stop teaching after we were married—"

"Excuse me?" Alan couldn't keep quiet any longer. A dozen things were churning inside him, raging to be spoken, but he carefully chose only one. "He was going to make you stop working?"

"No, he wasn't going to *make* me." Her tone was distinctly defensive. "But Peter was an important man, with an important job, and naturally we'd have to go where his work took him. Besides, I'd be too busy being his wife—"

"This is the twentieth century," Alan pointed out acerbically. "Didn't you ever hear of equal rights?"

"You don't understand!" Pam cried. And suddenly the tangled knot of emotions that she had pushed far down inside her began to unravel with alarming speed. Four hours ago she couldn't bear to talk about Peter, with Alan or anyone else, and now the words tumbled out and she couldn't stop them. "It wasn't just that—it was everything. Peter was too good for me, and I always knew it. He was smart, he was cosmopolitan, he was educated and ambitious— we came from two different worlds. I tried to be what he wanted me to but—I *like* it here, Alan! I like the mountains and the snow and the Rockies in the springtime. I like living in the same town I grew up in and knowing everybody's name and everybody's secrets, and I like being a lowly preschool teacher, and *that* was the problem, don't you see?"

She ran a harried hand through her bangs, casting briefly about the room as though looking for something to distract herself, but the dam was cracked and the words kept flooding through. "I don't *want* to climb the Matterhorn or ride in a limousine through Central Park—I like hearing about it, but I don't really want to do it, and Peter—that was where he belonged. I was outclassed from the beginning, and I was just too stupid to admit it."

Alan's voice was low but his eyes were carefully expressionless as he said, "It sounds as though he was the one who was outclassed."

Pam caught her breath, her fists clenched at her sides, and she opened her mouth for an instinctive defense of Peter. But it wouldn't come. Instead she swung away from the quiet truth in Alan's eyes, gripping the counter hard, and she said shakily, *"Damn him."*

It was as though the very words had given life to the rage that had been fulminating inside her, twisting and hiding and being denied so long. She closed her eyes tightly against it and every muscle in her body strained to hold it back, but it was no use. "Damn him!" she repeated, and her voice rose. "He had no right—all these years, all those promises—I built my life around that man! I tried to change for him, I waited for him, I planned for him—the bastard! He had no right!"

She was shaking and she couldn't help it; appalled by her own behavior, she desperately tried to clamp down on it but control evaded her grasp. She picked up Alan's glass from the sink, intending to wash it to give her hands something useful to do. But suddenly her hand tightened about the glass in a spasm of agonized fury; she turned and flung it against the wall.

"It's not fair!" she cried, and the tears broke through. She buried her face in her hands and sobbed.

Swiftly Alan was beside her, taking her shoulders and turning her gently to his chest. "It's all right, love," he said softly. "That's good. It's all right to cry...."

He held her and she wept helplessly. It was a long time before she realized that it was not pain that backed the tears, or even anger. It was relief.

Seven

———

5:40 p.m.

The minutes ticked by and Alan felt the world turn one slow, inevitable revolution as he held her in his arms. He knew, without analyzing it or wondering why, that this was what he had been waiting for since he had first met her. The last real and visible barrier had been dropped between them and beyond it was the wonder of what was yet to come. And it belonged only to them.

After her sobs diminished and her breathing evened, he kissed her hair, lightly, and tucked one loosened strand of it behind her ear. "How do you feel?"

"Foolish." Her tears had spent themselves, but her voice was still thick. "Exhausted. Free." The last word degenerated into almost a whisper, and her fingers involuntarily tightened themselves in the wool of his sweater. "Oh, Alan," she said miserably, "that was the worst part. When he told me it was over I was…glad. I guess I knew then that I had never really loved him."

Alan took a breath and closed his eyes. The backs of his fingers stroked her neck as he tried, very carefully, to find just the right words. "That's a two-way street, you know."

She nodded, slowly, against his chest, struggling to absorb the truths that were becoming clear to her. Peter had never loved her, any more than she loved him. There was nothing to mourn because there was nothing to miss. The only thing she failed to understand was how she could have mistaken Peter's self-motivated interest in her for love—the kind of love that could sustain a marriage, build a family, and last a lifetime.

How very strange it was that she had never realized what was missing in Peter until she met Alan.

She pushed away from Alan, a little disturbed by the comparison without knowing why. She wiped her hot, tear-dampened cheeks with both hands and forced a smile. "Well," she said, indicating the broken glass in the corner, "I guess we owe Mr. McMurty a glass."

As she moved away from him, Alan actually felt his hands ache with her absence and instinctively he moved as though to draw her back. But he stopped himself in time, and she did not see.

"I'll add one glass to my shopping list," he answered, trying to make his voice light.

Pam smiled nervously, pressing her palms briefly against her jeans, and turned toward the cabinet again. "I guess I'd better see about dinner."

She took one step, and then turned to face Alan, unable to keep up the pretense any longer. "Alan," she said. Her voice sounded a little strained, and there was an urgency pressing against her chest, a demanding tide of words that needed to be spoken. And she hardly knew where to begin. "Thank you. For... pestering me about Peter, and making me admit the truth. I know you did it on purpose, and—it was a good thing."

Alan smiled, somewhat uncertainly. "I don't seem to be able to do anything but good things when I'm with you."

Pamela felt her throat go tight, with nothing more than the sweetness of his smile. "That's what friends are for, aren't they? To make each other feel good about themselves?" And it was true. The only time she felt good—right, and whole, and completely at peace with herself—was when she was in Alan's arms.

Alan replied soberly, "I don't know. I've never had a real friend before."

Pam looked at him, the lanky, light-haired stranger who, only a day ago, had not even existed for her, and wonder flowed through her, concentrating in an ache that filled her heart. Because of him, her life would never be the same. He had touched parts of her no one had ever recognized before, he had opened her eyes to things inside herself even she had not known were there. No matter what happened now, he would always be a part of her. And the ache inside her strained toward him, yearning to find a way to tell him so.

She glanced briefly down at her interlaced hands and then looked at him again, hesitantly. "As long as we're on the subject of confessions—I have another one." She took a breath. "I was glad to be stuck here. If we had stayed by the cars we might have been found and—I didn't want to be rescued. All I could think about was what I was going to tell my family and friends and the way they would look at me, you know, out of the corners of their eyes when they thought I didn't notice, and what they would be thinking and— well, even being trapped in the middle of a blizzard was easier to deal with than that. So..." Anxiety crept into her tone and she tightened her fingers together. "I made sure I wouldn't have to face them any time soon. Are you mad at me?"

His smile was so easy and unfeigned that relief swept through Pamela like sunshine, dissolving the last lingering clouds of her uncertainty. "Do you think *I* wanted to be rescued?" he pointed out, extending his hands to her. "I've got a few problems waiting for me outside, too, you know."

Pam took two steps forward and her hands slipped into his gratefully. The smile in his eyes warmed her and drew her close. "Being snowbound in the wilderness *is* the best thing that ever happened to me," he told her, "in more ways than one."

For a long time they simply stood there, holding hands and sharing the kind of silent, unstrained communication that had become natural to them. Pamela couldn't say when the warmth in his eyes began to change, growing more subtle yet intense, nor when the quiet pleasure she felt at simply being with him quickened into something more. But she knew the transformation was mutual and inevitable, moving smoothly toward what could only be the next natural step.

Alan released her fingers and lifted his hand to touch her cheek, a tender, exploratory stroke that drew a sigh of pleasure from Pam. His fingers drifted to her jawline, tracing its shape, and followed the curve of her ear. A sparkling glow of warmth followed the course of his fingers to her throat and below.

Pam caught her breath as his fingers caressed her breast, a light, loving touch, but all the more erotic for its delicacy. His eyes never left her face, watching her reaction, the intensity of his gaze deepening and warming with her pleasure. Their hands were still entwined, and his lips softened with his own pleasure in the tender caress. Warmth penetrated the fabric of her sweater and her nipples tautened when his hand closed lightly over her shape; her heart caught and speeded with anticipation and the terrible, wonderful frustration of his gentle touch.

Her lips parted for breath and her fingers tightened on his, drawing him closer. Pam thought there had never been a sensation like this; never before had she looked into the eyes of a lover, captured in mind and body, while the pleasure he created for her was reflected back to him with simple, undisguised honesty. Only Alan could do this. Only with Alan was it possible.

He dropped his head and placed a long kiss on the curve of her neck. The palm of his hand flattened over her breast and his fingers tightened warmly as spirals of heat traveled from the touch of his lips to the very core of her abdomen, pulling threads of desire into an aching knot. Her legs lost their strength and she clutched at his upper arm with her free hand; her voice was barely a whisper. "Alan..."

There was no mistaking the need in her voice, and for a moment she felt the surge of reciprocal desire in Alan: the sharply indrawn breath, the tensing of his muscles as he tightened his embrace. And then, slowly, he moved away. His hand slid to her waist, where it rested lightly, hardly touching at all. He brushed the corner of her jaw with a petal-soft kiss, and then lifted his head. He said nothing, but the quiet question was in his eyes, and he waited patiently for an answer.

Pam knew she should turn away, move out of the circle of his embrace, away from his warmth and his heady scent and the all-too-ready temptation to just relax her body against him and let nature take its course. He was offering her the opportunity to do just that. And she tried, she really did.

She tried to think of all the reasons this was wrong, all the dangers it involved, all the regrets that would follow. She tried to remember that she had known him only briefly, that they would never meet again, that stress and shock were playing havoc with her judgment. She tried to do anything but look into the dark-silver mirror of his eyes, to think of anything except the way she felt when she was in his arms.

But she couldn't. All she wanted was to be with him, to be close to him, as close as she could possibly get and even more. She wanted the promise of his embrace to expand and be fulfilled, and she wanted it to last, if not forever, at least for this night. Her heart pounded and her breath grew short and even her skin ached with wanting it.

And he saw the answer in her eyes.

She said softly, "We're not doing this for the wrong reasons any more, are we?"

His eyes lightened, then darkened as he scanned her face, as though hardly daring to believe what he saw there. "I think," he answered, a little huskily, "that we were always . . . just making excuses."

"It shouldn't be," she felt compelled to whisper.

And he agreed immediately, "No, it shouldn't."

But this feeling might not ever come again, not ever in her life. This wonder, this delight, the joy of having discovered this man who could make her feel so right, so complete, might be hers only for this moment. And she couldn't turn away from it.

She smiled a little. Lifting her hand, she cupped it against his neck, delighting in the texture, the heat, the softness of his hair brushing the back of her hand, and enraptured by the pleasure that brightened his eyes with her touch. "All those reasons—they don't seem to matter any more, do they?"

"No," he whispered. And he kissed her.

Although the kiss started out as assurance, it was swiftly consumed in passion. The flame of wanting seemed to feed on itself and double, a sensory overload that raged unchecked as all their carefully maintained controls fell aside unnoticed. Neither of them was prepared for the unvarnished strength of mutual need, and it left them shaken, breathless and weak with parting.

Alan lifted an unsteady hand to her hair, smoothing down the errant strands of her braid his own searching hands had loosened. Her eyes were brilliant and drugged with passion, her face feverish to the touch. He felt as though he were drowning in her; his heart, his lungs, his bloodstream were all filled with her and yet he was hungry, starving for more. He had never known a need so overwhelming, so all-consuming, and it shook him to his very core. He wanted to clasp her to him and never let her go, he wanted to drink of her until his senses were reeling and then come back for more, he wanted to bury himself inside her, swiftly and completely and stay there forever, a part of her.

Somehow he managed to gesture toward the room. "I think," he said with difficulty, "that we can find some place more comfortable, don't you?"

Pam nodded, slipped her hand into his and together they walked to the bed.

A nervousness fluttered and tightened inside Pam's stomach with that simple act—not because she regretted her decision or was uncertain about what was to come. It was simply that it was all very new to her, and strange. She didn't recognize the woman who was accompanying this man to a stranger's bed; it wasn't the sort of thing Pamela Mercer did. She felt as if another mind were guiding her body and she was a jumble of conflicting thoughts and emotions inside.

But she needn't have worried. Alan didn't push. He sat upon the edge of the bed, one leg slightly bent at the knee, and with a gentle tug on her hand, he invited her to join him. And he said gently, "Believe it or not, I don't usually do this sort of thing, either."

Pam believed him. And the thoughtfulness behind the words caused her heart to swell again with that sweet, expansive emotion that felt so good. This was Alan, and she wasn't sorry.

She smiled. "This is weird, isn't it?" she admitted. "I don't seem to know what to do with my hands."

Alan grinned, looping his arms around her neck loosely, his forearms resting on her shoulders. "It'll come to you," he assured her.

Pam laughed a little, immediately relaxing. Alan's teasing grin faded into simple pleasure, and for a time they simply sat there, smiling at each other, enjoying the moment and growing used to the feeling.

Then Alan said, "I've been wanting to see your hair loose all afternoon. Do you mind?"

A little surprised, Pam shook her head.

Alan found the band that secured the end of her braid and slipped it off, careful not to snag. With his fingers he separated the thick, glossy strands and combed them free. Her hair was like satin against his fingertips, an exquisite tactile sensation that he wanted to savor to its fullest extent. Loosened, it fanned around her shoulders and draped in waves over her breasts like a luxuriant shawl, and for a moment he simply looked at her, filling his eyes with her loveliness.

"You are beautiful," he said softly.

He lifted a lock of her hair and brought it to his face, experiencing the texture of it against his skin, savoring the sweet, rich fragrance that enveloped him in her presence. "Ah, Pamela," he whispered. "I wish that I could give you even half the pleasure you give me, just by letting me look at you."

A smile of sheer happiness broke across Pam's face. She slid her hand around his neck, delighting in touching him, in merely being close to him. "Oh, Alan, you do. Without even trying—you do."

He released a soft breath and brought his forehead to rest against hers. "I want . . ." he said, but had difficulty finishing. So many things were bursting inside his head, so many things were clamoring inside his heart. "You are so special. I want to go slowly, and make this last."

Pam's lips brushed his cheek, and then clasped lightly on his neck. He tasted of warm masculinity and the faint tang of after-shave. "We have plenty of time."

He made a low sound of pleasure in his throat at the touch of her lips. His hands slid down her back, pressing her shape and drawing her closer, and Pam sank into his embrace as his mouth covered hers. *Time*, she thought dizzily. *All the time in the world.* . And she could spend all of it making love to him, slowly, thoroughly, and with exquisite anticipation, making it last forever.

His hands slipped beneath the hem of her sweater and she moaned softly as his fingers touched her bare skin, caressing her waist and her back. His own heavy sweater separated her from him, and when she pushed at the material impatiently he moved away from her for a moment and pulled it over his head.

Beneath the sweater he was wearing a cotton-knit shirt and as he started to unbutton it, Pamela stilled his fingers with her own. This was one pleasure she wanted to reserve for herself and, smiling, he dropped his hands.

His hair was tousled and gleaming in the shadowed light of the lantern, his eyes glowing yet so dark they were almost black. A thrill of expectation went through her as she looked at him, and her fingers were unsteady on the buttons at his throat. Her heart was beating loudly as one by one and with maddening difficulty each was loosened, revealing the golden luster of his skin, the sweep of his collarbone, a narrow triangle of chest. He let her do what she wanted, though she could see the slow, heavy rise and fall of his chest as she gathered the soft material in her hands and pulled it upward, over his head.

His chest was smooth, tapering to an athletic waist, his ribs banded with sinew, his shoulders curving into tight biceps. Pam drew in a deep breath and slid her hands over the sweep of his shoulders and down his arms. Leaning forward, she placed a kiss upon his chest. She felt his sharp intake of breath and the sensation of power was heady. Never before had she felt free to take the lead in lovemaking, to tantalize and enjoy and *play* at love. Simple delight caused a gurgle of laughter to form in her throat as she kissed him again and then, experimentally, darted her tongue over the flesh of his abdomen.

He gave a low gasp of pleasure and his hands tangled in her hair. She slid hers across his ribs, over the swell of his pectoral muscles and his flat nipples. She kissed him there and he moaned softly, his fingers tightening on her shoulders. "Not fair," he murmured.

"What?" she barely had breath for the word, so immersed was she in the sensory feast of his taste and texture and the intoxicating knowledge of his pleasure.

"This." Deftly he slid his hands beneath her sweater and pulled it upward. She moved away from him only long enough to allow the material to clear her head, and let him slip her bra off her shoulders.

He smiled at her. "Let me show you how wonderful that feels."

"It can't be as wonderful as making you feel good," she whispered, caressing his chest. But she was wrong.

His hands cupped her breasts and his fingertips stroked, light butterfly brushes that promised and aroused. He bent his head and his warm breath teased and whispered over her tight flesh, maddeningly close, suggesting and withholding and driving her to the peak of wanting. Her fingers tightened on his upper arms as his tongue stroked her nipple, sending darts of desire deep into her belly. Then his mouth closed upon her breast with warm, moist drawing motions and the fever flashed through her, draining her of strength and leaving her aching with need.

She sank back onto the mattress and his heat enveloped her like a cocoon. His hand closed upon her jeaned thigh and his lips left her breast, traveling with stabbing flames of pleasure to her ribs and the sensitive flesh of her abdomen. His hand moved upward until it pressed gently against the apex of her thighs, where a flood of liquid heat met his touch. A cry caught in her throat and she went still with the sensation, rapt with expectation and need.

He lifted his head and greedily she sought his mouth, her hands roaming over the muscles of his back, the frustrating band of material at his waist, the firmness of his buttocks. He entwined one leg with hers and they shifted onto their sides. She hardly knew when he unsnapped her jeans and separated the zipper. She only knew the electrifying sensation of his hand, flat against her naked abdomen, and his fingers slipping inside the elastic of her panties.

His touch was like silk on her secret flesh, tender, gliding strokes that caressed rather than probed. The roar of her heart all but exploded in Pam's head, and she forgot to breathe. Alan's mouth left hers and, irrationally, she tried to hide her face from him. But with his other hand he stroked her cheek, and watched her eyes as he slowly slipped one finger inside her.

The blaze of pleasure in his eyes must have reflected her own. She saw only the blur of his flushed, damp face and heard a muffled cry that could have been her own as she instinctively arched her hips forward. He moved deeper and then, with exquisite care and agonizing slowness, withdrew.

Pam clung to him, trembling, her mouth open against his shoulder drawing in his scent and his taste. He caught her head between his hands, threading his fingers through her hair, and their mouths met in a

kiss that was hot and dizzying, insatiable in its de-
mand. Impatiently, he pushed her jeans and her panties down over her hips and Pam, with her head
spinning and her heart pounding, was too disoriented
to help him. She didn't understand why he had
stopped until he brought his face back to hers and said
softly, "Pamela . . . your boots."

For a moment she was confused and then, understanding, an incredulous giggle bubbled up inside her.
What a strange and wonderful feeling it was when
passion mixed with laughter. How delightful to be reminded, even in the midst of intimacy, that they could
still enjoy one another in the simplest ways.

Alan leaned over her, the sound of her laughter
mixing with the passion in his eyes. "You think it's
funny, do you?" He caught her hair in both hands and
drew it over her face, crisscrossing locks in a light rope
across her throat. "Then *you* take them off. Unless,
of course, you'd rather spend the rest of the night
tangled up in those things."

Pam pushed her hair away from her eyes and her
mouth and spent a moment simply reveling in the sight
of his face above her, flushed and damp and gentled
with amusement, as familiar as her own reflection and
as welcome as a sunrise. Alan, adoring and adored,
hers alone.

"That doesn't sound like much fun," she admitted
breathlessly.

She sat up to tug off her boots, and kicked aside her
jeans. She returned to him naked and aglow with the
quick light of wonder and admiration that flared in his

eyes, but when he reached for her she stopped him with a hand laid lightly against his chest. "Wait."

She felt his sharply indrawn breath and the tightening of the muscles of his abdomen as she loosened the button of his trousers and slid down the zipper. She had never undressed a man before and the sense of discovery, of anticipation mixed with shyness, made her hands tremble and her pulse pound. Her fingertips brushed the hard, heated length of him, at first accidentally, and then, experimentally, more deliberately. The intense expression of concentrated pleasure that softened his face was like a surge of energy to her core. She pushed his clothing downward and when it was discarded she knelt between his naked thighs, her hands exploring the tight musculature of his legs, and upward to the center of him where she held his power, for a moment, cupped in her hand.

His breathing was slow and deep and hot against her shoulder; his hands caressed her back. He moved one leg around her, cradling and guiding her as he lowered her to the bed. He rested his weight on his elbows and his hands cupped her face, his body covering her like a blanket. Lost in the depths of his gaze, it seemed to Pam that more than her body cried out for him. Her mind, her soul, the very essence of her being ached with emptiness and begged to be filled by him.

Instinctively her legs settled on either side of him and he dropped a kiss on each of her eyelids, his breath fanning across her face like a caress. A sharp flare of awareness registered his pressure against her tender, aching flesh, poised for entrance. Her hands tightened on his back and she lost her breath as he pushed a little way in. The intensity of the sensation drew a small gasp from her, and he held himself there, the muscles of his arms tense and straining, while she became accustomed to him, and the strangeness of his presence. And then he lowered his lips to hers, lightly touching, and on a shared breath, he pushed fully inside her.

Even Pam's heartbeat seemed to be suspended, every sense rapt and intense with his penetration; the empty part of her expanding and opening, filling with him. Her fingers tightened on his shoulders and even the pores of her skin seemed to absorb his texture, becoming a part of him. And when he was buried deeply within her the agony of wanting transformed itself into a flood tide of joy, of completeness, of wonder so intense that even this exquisite act of joining could not express it fully.

She felt his unsteady fingertips stroking her cheek and heard the whisper of her name, and when she looked at him the wonder and delight in his eyes redoubled her own. She wrapped her arms around him and held him tightly, closing her eyes against the beauty of the moment which was almost too much for her to contain.

How could anything this wonderful ever happen to me? she thought dazedly. *I don't deserve anything so perfect as this* . . . And yet the spiraling happiness within her was only the beginning, and by its very nature demanded more, straining and stretching to capture forever. The rhythms that moved them were thoughtless and eternal, a rhapsody of body and soul, each stroke promising more, drawing her closer to the edge of what it seemed she had waited her whole life to claim. And when the tension inside her became unbearable, she cried out and clung to him as, with one great plunge he drove himself deep inside her and the waves of fulfillment began to break. She lost cognizance and will, helpless against the cascades of breathless wonder where nothing existed except Alan...Alan and herself, perfectly, permanently blended into one.

For that single, timeless instant she held the future in her hands and she knew, as she had never known anything before, that this was the way it was meant to be. Even as the colors of ecstasy faded and the scorching heat of passion gave way to a contented glow, she knew that the one thing she had been searching for all her life had been hers tonight. And though a small voice warned her of pain to come, she fiercely refused to listen. She wrapped her arms around Alan and held him tight and though she knew it wasn't true, it felt like forever. And that was enough.

Eight

The wind buffeted the walls of the cabin and outside there was a splintering and crashing sound as another heavy limb fell beneath the weight of the snow. Pam smiled drowsily against Alan's chest, his heartbeat strong and steady beneath her ear. He had found a quilt on the blanket chest at the foot of the bed and drawn it over them, and they lay inside that cozy nest, their legs entwined and their hands lazily stroking, still dazed by what they had shared.

"Oh, Alan," Pam murmured. "Do you feel as wonderful as I do?"

Alan took a breath, but the frailty of words left him helpless. Though his body was drained his thoughts were spinning, his head bursting with things he wanted to tell her. How was he feeling? The emotions that swelled up inside him left him weak, awed with his own inability to express. He wanted to hold her, to press her to him until her very skin became fused with his, to breathe in her essence, to make her an indelible part of him. He wanted to be inside her thoughts, to know and absorb everything that was her, to drink her in like water on dry earth.

He wanted to open his eyes and see her face every morning for the rest of his life; to spend his days never more than an arm's reach from her, to carry her laughter inside his head and her scent on his skin and her taste on the back of his tongue like an exotic delicacy whose flavor never faded. He had never wanted like this, with such intense, all-consuming, magnificent certainty. And how could he tell her that? The fierce possessiveness of his emotions overwhelmed him, and he couldn't put them into words.

He dropped his face to her hair and released a long breath. "I feel," he said, lying back and drawing her close, "like no one ever made love before in the history of the world, until you and I. I feel like my heart only started beating an hour ago and I don't even remember living before I met you. Everything is sparkling. I can hear the snow fall. I've got this funny pain in my chest and I just now realized it's because I'm so happy I can hardly breathe. I feel like I'm floating." He smiled down at her. "How about you?"

The delirious, escalating joy inside her bubbled up into a laugh of sheer exhilaration. She caught both his hands in hers and slid on top of him, stretching his arms over his head, savoring the full length of his body for one dazzling moment. She looked down at him, her eyes dancing and her skin tingling. Her hair formed a soft veil on either side of his face, sealing them together.

"Oh, Alan, I feel like I could sprout wings and fly!"

He chuckled low in his throat, but his eyes were busy on her face, adoring and delighting in each of her separate features. "Glad to accommodate you."

She laughed again, just because it felt good to laugh and because he was so beautiful and she was so happy. But as the laughter faded poignancy caught in her chest and she said softly, "I never expected this, did you?"

His eyes were deep and tender and love-drowsed. "How could I? No one could imagine this. But looking back, it almost seems inevitable, doesn't it?"

"That we'd make love?"

"That we'd find each other in a snowstorm, that we'd know each other and show each other things no one else could. And that when we made love, it would somehow be more than that."

Pamela dropped her eyes, shielding from him the sudden intensity of emotion she could not even understand, much less share. Yes, it was more than making love, what they had known. Yet it shouldn't be. It couldn't be.

Alan said, "I'd kiss you if you let go of my hands."

Her lips curved into a teasing smile as she looked down at him. "You can kiss me without your hands."

"I'm not sure I know how."

"Try."

"It doesn't sound like much fun."

She lowered her face, brushing his lips with her own and tantalizing him with darts of her tongue, playfully at first. She traced the shape of his mouth with the tip of her tongue and delicately tasted the inside, the silky texture of his inner lip and the smoothness of his teeth.

Their breaths melded and fanned a flame between them as he opened his mouth and she took it with her own. His tongue penetrated the moist inner recesses of her mouth in a sensuous replication of the mating they had just shared, a thorough, demanding exploration that left her skin aflame and her pulse pounding. She felt him growing hard and heated against her thigh, and that sensation sent a rush of glory to her head, a renewed aching and tingling to her loins.

"That was pretty good," she said breathlessly, "without your hands."

He smiled at her. "Are you tired?"

She whispered, "No."

His fingers tightened on hers and the muscles of his arms flexed as he pushed her upward to a sitting position and, guiding her with his eyes and arms, down until she felt the strength of his sex centered between her thighs. Her breathing was slow and unsteady and the pounding of her heart blurred her vision; her grip on Alan's hands grew weak as she lifted her hips slightly and then, slowly, took him inside her.

The sensation was different but, if possible, even more intense. Her senses focused sharply, riveted in concentration upon the firm upward pressure. Her head roared and her breath was shallow, her heart thundering against her ribs. Her muscles were tense, and she kept her eyes closed. "I've never done this before," she whispered.

Alan's hands settled around her waist, easing some of her weight. "Take it easy," he advised softly. "Are you uncomfortable?"

She drew in a breath and shook her head, then, shyly, she opened her eyes. His face was tender, yet rapt with the same kind of suspended attention she was feeling, suffused in pleasure. She smiled at him. "It's wonderful," she murmured, "looking down at your face. Now I can watch your eyes."

"Yes." A dazed smile softened his face as he brought his hands to her breasts. "And I can do this."

The sweet, drawing motions of his fingers on her breasts were a maddening, delightful stimulant, sending weakening waves of pleasure through her limbs. The tension left her muscles only to be replaced by a new kind of alertness as she let her weight press down on him and felt him sink deep into her, deeper than she had ever imagined he could be, so deep that she gasped.

"Pamela?" His eyes were quick with concern, his touch tender upon her cheek.

She drew in a deep, expansive breath, arching her neck backward, and shook her head. "Oh, Alan," she breathed. "This is the way it was meant to be, isn't it? Life and love and everything."

"Yes."

She looked into his face, and saw the adoration in his eyes, and she thought it couldn't get any better than this.

But it did.

* * *

9:00 p.m.

They made a meal of instant oatmeal and canned peaches and ate it sitting up in the freshly made bed. Alan had found a shirt in his duffel bag for Pam to wear, and it was white silk. She felt pampered and contented and adored, like a character from a fairy tale.

"This isn't my life," she decided dreamily. She set her bowl aside and pulled the quilt over her shoulders, snuggling against Alan. "It's something somebody made up."

Alan put his arm around her shoulders, settling back against the pillows. "I made it up," he told her. "This is all a dream I'm having and you just happen to be in it."

She chuckled sleepily. "You're pretty good at dreaming."

"One of my best things," he admitted immodestly. "Let me dream one for you. Think of a place you'd like to be, any place in the world. I'll take you there."

The lantern had been extinguished and the room was lit only by a small candle on the table beside the bed. The wind had died down to a distant sigh and the fire in the stove murmured and crackled happily. It was easy to imagine, effortless to pretend, simple to believe that life would go on like this, secure and peaceful and uninterrupted in Alan's arms, for a millenium or more.

She reached for his hand beneath the quilt, lacing her fingers with his and resting them against his bare abdomen. She liked the feel of his skin against her hand, warm and familiar and exclusively hers.

"Umm . . . Alpha Centauri."

He gave her a reproachful look. "I said in the *world*."

"You didn't specify planet Earth."

"How can I take you somewhere I've never been before?"

She glanced up at him teasingly. "I think you already have."

His eyes softened as he captured a strand of her hair and wound it around his index finger. "I think you're right."

"Okay." She settled her head against his shoulder, finding the most comfortable position, and decided, "The South Pacific."

"Tahiti. Okay, close your eyes. It's nighttime, you're on the beach. It's a long, white beach, lined with torches along the shore side, and the torches kind of sway back and forth with the breeze. There's a moon, and more stars in the sky than you've ever seen in your life, but if you look at them long enough you realize they aren't familiar stars; they're all in the wrong places, and that's exciting. You feel like you're on an exotic adventure.

"Their air doesn't smell like salt and fish, like it does on American beaches. It's clean and fresh, with an undertaste of something spicy, like tropical perfume. The surf sounds like someone sighing in the background, and the ocean is the clearest, deepest royal blue you've ever seen. The sand beneath your feet is still warm. . . ."

Pam smiled beneath her closed eyes, seeing it, feeling it. "What am I wearing?"

"You're wearing a white dress, full and billowy. Your hair is loose, like it is now, and the breeze ruffles your skirt and your hair, tickling your face. You can hear Polynesian music from the hotel in the background, and you think this is the most romantic place in the world, and it would be perfect if only there were someone to share it with you . . . and then I walk up."

He leaned down and kissed the top of her head, his hand caressing her shoulder. "I don't say anything, I just smile at you. And then I put my arm around your waist and we walk together, just the two of us with the surf and the moon and the breeze that smells like tropical flowers, and you're happier than you've ever been in your life. So am I."

"Oh, Alan." She couldn't say any more. She lay against him with her eyes closed and the vision lingering in her head and she thought, *What an incredible man he is. Has there ever been anyone like him?* And how could it be possible that she, of all people, had attracted the attention of a man like this? She didn't deserve this. Such things never happened to Pamela Mercer, and it could not be real.

But, oh, it was glorious pretending.

"London," she sighed contentedly against his shoulder. "Take me to London."

"It's raining," he responded immediately, "a light, warm springtime rain, and you're standing at a bus stop. Not all in a mass, like people do here, but in a straight line, because British people are very orderly. There's a building behind you with windowboxes full of red and yellow tulips. The streets are crowded with little cars and big red buses, and you can smell exhaust fumes, wet streets. The people around you are all talking in strange accents, and you're getting soaked because you've forgotten your umbrella, which immediately marks you as a tourist and brings out the best of British snobbery. You're feeling kind of lonely and homesick, and then suddenly I'm there, opening my umbrella for you.''

A delighted smile curved her lips as she snuggled deeper into the hollow of his shoulder. "And then we go back to your flat where you build a fire in a tiny, little fireplace and serve me tea and crumpets.''

"No. We go to the St. Georges hotel, where I have a suite. I run a bath for you in the big marble tub and sprinkle the water with bath salts that smell like herbs and sandalwood and turn the water aqua blue. And afterward you wrap yourself in a towel as thick and soft as lambs' wool, and dry your hair before the fireplace while I sit beside you, thinking how beautiful you are.''

She laughed softly, suffused with the pleasure he had created for her. "It's wonderful,'' she murmured, and extracted her fingers from his to stretch her arms around him, hugging him. ''*You*'re wonderful.''

He shifted position so that he was leaning over her, and took her face in his hands. His eyes were very serious, slightly fevered with the certainty of a promise. "I can take you there, Pamela. London, Tahiti, Rome, the Scottish Highlands...there's an island in the Caribbean that can only be reached by private plane, and we can have it to ourselves for as long as we want. Anything, any place in the world, it's yours. All you have to do is ask.''

And there it was, desperate reality creeping on tentacled fingers into their cozy paradise. He meant it. Pamela Mercer, with her J.C. Penney wardrobe and her sensible shoes, jetting off to Tahiti or Rome or a private Caribbean island with a man whose middle name she didn't even know. Impossibilities, impracticalities and absurdities surged forward, pounding at the walls of their secure shelter with demanding fists.

She said, trying to force lightness into her tone, ''I thought you were broke.''

Impatience—or perhaps it was a plea—shadowed his eyes. ''Pamela...''

But she would not give him the answer he wanted. She refused to let the dream end. Not now, not yet.

She closed her eyes, wrapping her arms around him, and said softly, ''I don't want to go to any of those places. I want you to take me to a cabin in the Rocky Mountains, with a blizzard raging outside and a big bed with eiderdown quilts...''

After a moment, the tension left his muscles and he relaxed beside her. His hands played in her hair and his breath was soft on her cheek while she spun her dream for him. They made love in slow, tender silence, and after a long time, they slept.

Saturday, 7:00 a.m.

When Pamela awoke, it was cold. Instinctively she snuggled closer to Alan, burrowing her head under the quilts. He smelled of sleepy masculinity and her, and

drowsily she registered how remarkable it was to
awake with the remnants of a dream still clinging to
the corners of her mind and realize that it wasn't a
dream, at all: Alan's warm, strong body was still
wrapped around her, Alan's breathing was still a
whisper in her ear, Alan was still hers. And she sa-
vored the moment, knowing that soon she must awake
and it might all disappear.

Alan stirred and made a soft sound, stretching out
his legs and then wrapping them around her again.
"It's cold," he murmured.

She didn't open her eyes. "I know."

"And quiet."

Pamela hadn't noticed before, but he was right. The
wind had stopped roaring, the windowpanes no longer
rattled, and there was no cracking and groaning of tree
limbs outside. The stillness made her uneasy, drawing
her to a fuller stage of wakefulness.

"Is it morning?"

"I think so."

"Too bad."

Her knee was between his legs and she could feel his
sleepy, half-aroused state against her. The temptation
was to let her hands and her lips wander, to bring them
both to wakefulness in the way they had fallen asleep.
But the bite of the air was cold on her ears and her
nose, and morning was waiting. Reluctantly, she extracted herself from him.

He made a sound of protest and reached for her
drowsily. "Don't get up."

"I have to check the fire."

"Sounds like a man's job to me."

She could not remember a morning when she was smiling before she fully opened her eyes, but that was unmistakably what she was doing now. "To me, too. But I think I'll check the fire before we both freeze. Besides, I have to go to the bathroom."

"In that case..." He turned over and pulled the covers over his head.

Pam shivered as she got out of bed and searched for her jeans and a pair of socks to protect her feet from the icy hardwood floor. Rubbing her arms furiously against the chill, she padded over to the stove. The fire hadn't completely died down, but the few grayish embers inside the stove were throwing off precious little heat. She carefully fed the sparks a handful of kindling and added the last two logs, then hurried to the bathroom while the fire caught.

A nice blaze was going when she returned, so she closed the door and adjusted the vents. And then there was no putting it off any longer. She went through the kitchen to the back door and peered outside.

She caught her breath at what she saw. A wall of snow that reached almost to her chest blocked her exit, but beyond it the sky was pale gray and still. No snow fell, no wind blew. The storm was over.

A chill crept upon her, and a hollow feeling settled inside her stomach for which she had no rational explanation. She had never expected it to last forever. She had always known morning would come, and the storm would pass away. For every beginning there was an ending. Nothing lasted forever.

When she returned Alan was already dressed, sitting on the side of the bed and lacing up his borrowed boots. He looked up at her, and immediately his expression changed. "What's wrong?"

Pam smiled quickly, though the effort seemed to stretch her face. She linked her hands tightly together before her and said, "Nothing. As a matter of fact, the good news is, the snow has stopped."

Alan stared at her. If the snow had stopped, the worst was over. They could get out of here, find a telephone, rescue their cars and be on their way. That was what they had been waiting for, hoping for. Then why did he feel as if he had a lead weight in the pit of his stomach?

Pam searched his eyes anxiously, afraid to interpret what she saw there. She added hesitantly, "Of course, the bad news is that there's about three feet of snow blocking the door. It won't be so easy to get out of here."

Alan felt hope, faint and frail, begin to stir again. Deliberately, he finished tying his boots and stood. "Well, then," he said, with far more enthusiasm than he felt, "I guess we'd better go see what we can do."

Alan determined that the wall of snow did not appear to be horizontally regular, but sloped downward slightly beyond the door. Though he knew that to have hoped otherwise was foolish—they would soon freeze without firewood—he couldn't suppress an irrational stab of disappointment that escape was going to be so easy.

Alan brought up a kitchen chair for Pam to stand on, and eased her over the snow mound and outside. He followed a few seconds later. The snow was not very tightly packed, causing him to flounder a little before he slid down the incline to join Pam. Apparently the wind had blown heavy drifts all around the house, but they weren't really sealed in at any point. And it wasn't nearly as cold as it had been yesterday.

Pam was brushing the snow off the bottom of her jeans and he trudged the few feet to stand beside her. The ground was not entirely firm beneath his feet and his legs sank calf-deep into snow at some points, so it was slow going. They spent a few moments looking around and getting their bearings, not speaking.

So here we are, Alan thought unhappily, shoving his hands deep into the pockets of the lumberman's jacket. *Out in the big, wide world again. Free.* Could it have been only last night that he prayed for the snow to stop?

He looked hopefully at the pale sky. "It might start snowing again."

"It might," Pam agreed. But she didn't like the look of those clouds. They were too high and light, and they looked as though they might separate into clear, blue sky at any moment.

She ventured a glance at him, wondering what he was thinking. He was the one who had been so anxious to leave yesterday, raving about cabin fever and being trapped. Of course he wouldn't want to stay here one minute longer than necessary, carrying wood to keep warm and eating out of cans; no one in his right mind would. She had a cozy, electrically heated home waiting for her not ten miles down the road, with a hot shower, clean clothes and her mother's apple spice cake warm from the oven. And that was where she belonged, not hiding up here in a cabin that didn't belong to her, waiting for . . . what?

She cleared her throat and spoke up reluctantly. "Of course, if we're going to leave we should do it now. If the snow is this deep here it's going to be worse going down the hill, and who knows what kind of fallen trees and such we'll find. It could take a while just to get back to the cars."

"Yes," he said slowly. He hunched his shoulders miserably and let his eyes travel over the blank white landscape. How could it be only yesterday that they had struggled against the wind and the snow to find this place? Could only a handful of hours have passed since he had first taken her in his arms and shared a kiss that shouldn't have been . . . but had changed everything? It was too soon. Everything was happening too soon.

He looked at her abruptly, his tone severe. "You can't seriously be considering going back through those woods in this mess. Look, it's over my boots right where we're standing. We could break a leg."

She seized on hope and held fast. "The roads are probably still closed. It's not as though we could go anywhere."

"I can't even get my car started—even if we could dig it out from under the snow."

"And nobody's looking for us. I mean, we're not worrying anyone by being gone."

"How can they look? A person would have to be crazy to try to get on the roads today."

"It's really not safe, and we have plenty of food—"

"We can dig a path to the woodshed—"

"The smartest thing to do is just stay here. At least for a while."

They looked at each other, and it seemed they breathed a single simultaneous breath of relief which easily and naturally turned into a shared smile. The problem wasn't solved; they both knew that. But it was postponed, and they had found a way to hold on to the most important thing: a little more time.

Nine

So what does your brother do?'' Alan asked, spreading more processed cheese on his cracker.

"Jerry?'' Pam tipped the last few drops of the second bottle of wine into her glass. "He sells used cars over in Summerville. Actually, he's a partner in the dealership. He and his wife have a great big house on a hill, with a swimming pool.''

They were lounging on opposite ends of the sofa, their legs crossed over each other's, snacking on soda crackers and a jar of cheese spread Alan had found in the back of the cabinet. They had spent the morning usefully occupied clearing a path to the woodshed with the shovel they had found in the utility shed, and lunch had been foregone for lovemaking, which carried with it a frenetic quality that was both powerful and a little frightening. They tried to pretend nothing had changed, and yet it was there, haunting them. Even the shutters that Pam had pried open were a constant reminder that a world was out there waiting for them in the late-afternoon sunlight; sooner or later they would have to go out to meet it.

Yet between them it was never acknowledged. They talked about anything and everything else: his life, her life, philosophy and fantasy, but even their conversation had a desperate, hungry edge to it, as though they were storing up memories for the time to come. Pamela knew that was exactly what she was doing. Soon the memories would be all she would have of him, and she wanted them to be crisp and alive and vivid in every detail.

"Where do you live?" she asked, and realized once it was spoken how inane that question sounded. After all she had shared with this man, she did not even know that much about him. She felt sad, and unaccountably lonely.

But Alan did not seem to find anything unusual in the inquiry. "Cambridge," he answered, popping the cracker into his mouth.

"Massachusetts? As in Harvard?"

"Um-hm. It snows there, too, but I try not to be there when it does."

"Which is why you were in California."

"Right."

"Do you have one of those big old houses with gables and beveled-glass windows?"

"No. I have an efficiency apartment off-campus. I've never been in one place long enough to have a house."

"What's it like?" she asked curiously, trying to picture him there.

"Like all efficiency apartments off-campus." To his surprise, Alan found that he could not remember much about it. Everything in his life had been colorless and nondescript, like a series of hotel rooms where nothing ever changed but the view, until he met Pamela. And from this moment on she would remain the only spot of color in a neutral world, the center from which all things gravitated. Nothing would ever be the same because of her.

"Alan?"

He smiled quickly and brought his attention back to her question. "White walls, brown carpet...and books. Lots of books. And a bicycle."

She laughed. "A bicycle? Just like a regular student?"

"I am a regular student. Besides, it keeps me in shape."

Conversation faltered, but this time the silence had a heaviness to it, almost an emptiness. For the past six hours they had filled up that emptiness with words in a desperately energetic attempt to keep the future at bay. He knew every detail about the small town in which she lived, the two-story clapboard house she shared with her parents and younger sister, the preschool in which she worked with the rainbow over the door and the students who called her "Miss Pam" and brought her crayon drawings and crushed bouquets of

wildflowers. She knew about his childhood play-
mates, his travels, his studies. A world still yawned
between them.

As if with one mind, they were compelled once
again to try to bridge that gap.

"Do you—"

"Tell me about—"

They broke off, offering weak, apologetic smiles
that faded into bleakness for the futility of the effort.
Pam lowered her eyes to her wineglass, and then Alan
said suddenly, "Come with me, Pamela."

She looked up at him, startled. "To Cambridge?"

"Anywhere. Yes, back to Cambridge. Why not? We
could get an apartment there while I finish my doctorate, you could even teach if you want to. And afterward—"

"Alan." She averted her eyes.

"All right, then." He leaned forward, closing his
hand around her calf, and there was urgency in his
voice, and his touch. "I'll stay here with you. I know
you don't want to leave your job, and your folks.
That's all right, I can stay. I have no place else to go,
Pamela, if you're not with me."

Her throat convulsed suddenly, and she drew a
shaky breath. She made herself look at him and tried,
desperately, to keep her voice light. "I can't just—
move in with a man I hardly know."

He smiled, though it looked rather stiff, trying to
follow her cue. His fingers loosened their grip on her
leg and she could see him forcing herself to relax.
"Which is entirely different from spending a week-

end of passion and life-or-death adventure with a man you hardly know, right?''

"Right." Her voice was husky, and she took a quick sip of wine to clear it. But the liquid felt bitter in her throat, and she could hardly swallow.

His expression was deliberately mild, and so was his tone, but his eyes were alert to her every movement. "Recent studies show that the average married couple spends less than three hours a week talking to each other. We've known each other twenty-nine hours and we've spent every minute of that time—well, almost—talking. Which means we now know each other as well as people who have been married three months."

She managed a smile. "The honeymoon isn't even over yet."

"No," he answered softly. "It's barely even begun."

His eyes held hers for a long moment, and though she tried, desperately she tried, she could not fight back the looming shadow of reality any longer. She was not a fairy princess, she was not a character in someone else's dream; she was plain, old Pamela Mercer and it was time to let the fantasy go.

She swung her feet to the floor and stood up. "Alan, it's like this." She took a breath and tried to look at him but found that she couldn't. She walked a few steps away, her eyes focused on the sweeping panorama of snow outside the window...so vast, so white, so empty. Even until she spoke she did not know how difficult it would be, nor how much it would hurt.

"Monday morning I go back to work. I'll wake up in the same room I've woken up in for twenty-five years, I'll fight with my sister over the bathroom, I'll get dressed in a hurry because I'm late and I'll drink half a cup of coffee and get in my car and drive five miles to school where over a dozen children will be jumping up and down trying to tell me about their weekend, then I'll spend the day wiping noses and pouring juice and trying to make the alphabet sound like the most exciting thing in the world and the next day I'll do it all over again because that's my life and I like it."

Both hands were wound tightly about her wineglass, so tightly that her shoulders ached. She stared blindly into the liquid and saw nothing but her reflection there—pale, strained and featureless. "And you . . . you'll straighten out your problems with the police and your father, and then you'll go back to Massachusetts and you'll finish your degree because it's something you have to do, and you told me yourself you always finish what you start. And in the summer maybe you'll go looking for polar bears in Alaska or shark fishing in Australia because that's *your* life, don't you see?"

The silence lasted the space of two long, aching heartbeats. Then Alan said very quietly behind her, "You can't mean that we're just going to leave this place and—forget about each other."

No! She wanted to scream the word with all the power, all the agony in her soul. Forget about Alan? The very concept was unimaginable. He was as firmly woven inside the fabric of her being as threads of a cloth, inextricable, a part of the whole. The memory of him, and the presence of him in the secret, carefully guarded chamber of her heart was something she would live with for the rest of her life. But . . .

"No." Her voice was barely a whisper, choked and thick. "No, we won't forget about each other. You—are the most important thing that's ever happened to me, Alan, and this time with you is something no one can take away from me, ever."

She turned to him, and the anguish she felt was a plea for him to understand—or to somehow, some way, convince her that she was wrong. "Alan, don't you see? This weekend, what we've shared—it was just an interlude, two days out of thousands of days in a person's life, and though they were the most special, perfect days I've ever known, they can't make any difference, not in the long run, not in the real world. Everything is the same out there, nothing has changed. *We*'re still the same, with separate lives and separate responsibilities and it just *can't make any difference.*"

Alan's heart was beating so laboriously that it hurt his chest, and he could not take a deep breath. He said hoarsely, "I can't believe you're doing this."

He saw the pain cross her face, but it was only a reflection, a dim and distant image of his own. Somewhere deep inside a small voice was nagging at him, insisting that she was right, telling him to listen, demanding how he could blame her when she was only telling the truth. But he refused to listen to that voice, and his only defense against it was anger.

"I can't believe you're doing this," he repeated, more forcefully, and he stood up. "Don't you know what you mean to me, what you've done to me? And now you want me to just walk away from you and pretend it never happened?"

She closed her eyes against the agony that washed over her and shook her head mutely. And though her pain went through Alan like a knife, he couldn't seem to stop himself from hurting her more.

"It already *has* made a difference, don't you see that?" He wanted to go to her and take her by the shoulders, to grip her hard and make her look at him, to force her to see the truth that was so clear to him. But the fury inside him was too raw and demanding, and he made himself walk away from her, running his fingers tightly through his hair as he desperately fought for calm. "Nothing inside me will ever be the same because of you and you want me to believe it's *over*, just like that?"

"I don't want it to be over!" she cried.

Suddenly he whirled on her. "I think you do. I don't think it has anything to do with who we are or what's waiting for us outside. I think you're just afraid of making another mistake. You've got us all mixed up in your mind—your Peter with his important ambitions and limo rides in the park, and me. Well, I'm not Peter!"

He crossed the room and gripped her arm with such abruptness and such ferocity that the wineglass she held shattered on the floor. Her eyes met his, wild with torment, but he was beyond caring, almost beyond noticing. "Did you ever feel about Peter the way you feel about me?'' he demanded. ''Did you ever know with Peter what you've known with me? Did you?''

''No!'' she cried, and suddenly his mouth covered hers.

They came together in fierce possessiveness and ragged need, their lovemaking desperate and hungry as they strove to capture what was, even then, slipping from their grasp. And even when their bodies were exhausted, they clung together, still joined, trying to pretend that the physical unity they shared could change the world, could somehow make everything all right, and that it would last forever.

After a long time Alan moved away from her, holding her lightly in his arms. She was very still, her hand curled against his chest, her breathing soft. His mind was racing, searching, dodging the shadows that leapt out at him and desperately trying to find some way to evade the truth...but he couldn't. It weighed down upon him like a powerful force, it blocked his every move. She was right. There was nothing for them outside this time, this place. The bleakness of that reality wrapped itself around him like a shroud.

What could he offer her? As the heir to a fortune, he could offer her exotic places, luxurious gifts, glamour and prestige...all the things she didn't want. As the rebellious son of a ruthless millionaire he could offer her unemployment, uncertainty and incompetence. There was no place for her in his world, nor for him in hers. With all his soul he wanted to believe otherwise; he wanted to tell her that he would change, his life would change, he would carve a place for them with his bare hands if he had to...but deep inside he knew himself too well. The habits of a lifetime would creep back upon him, and the security of routine choices were as deeply embedded in his psyche as they were in hers. There were no promises he could make her.

He turned to her, and he thought his heart would break, just with looking at her. "I'm in love with you, Pamela," he said simply.

"I know." Her arms tightened around him and one sluggish tear rolled down her cheek and splashed on his chest. "I love you, too. I guess…that's what makes it hurt so much."

Sunday, 9:10 a.m.

They were gathering firewood the next morning when they heard the helicopter overhead. Collecting wood was a somewhat futile gesture because they both knew that, whatever happened, they would somehow have to start making their way back to the real world today. And though every minute they spent together was only prolonging the pain, they still held on, blindly and desperately, to every last moment.

Pam squinted into the bright blue sky, then gasped as she saw the Raintree County Sheriff's Department logo on the side of the helicopter. She dropped the firewood and began to wave frantically, jumping up and down. "It's my dad!" she shouted to Alan. "He's found us."

The helicopter dropped in acknowledgment, then banked and began to move away.

"He's leaving!"

"They can't land here," Pam explained. The sound of chopper blades faded and she turned to Alan, the full significance of what had just happened settling over her like a damp fog. It was over. There was no more avoiding it, no more postponing it. It was over.

"It will take them a while to climb back up here," she said. Her voice was strained.

For a moment Alan's face held no expression, at all. And then he managed a bleak smile. "Well. We'd better start getting this place straightened up, then."

They worked in silence, washing dishes, stripping the bed, sweeping and replacing the dust covers, stacking the firewood neatly on the hearth. Alan gathered up his things—the shirt that smelled like her, the sweater she had wept against when she told him about Peter—and stuffed them in his duffel bag. He put the jacket and boots in the closet just as he had found them, and Pam folded the emergency blankets she had taken from her car, and picked up her flashlight. At last there was nothing for them to do but stand in the center of the room and look around.

"Well," Pam said with forced brightness, almost brittleness, in her tone. "You'd hardly know we'd been here."

"No, you wouldn't," agreed Alan, and there had never been a more desolate feeling in the world than to stand in that room where the whole panorama of his life had been played and to see with his own eyes that nothing had changed. It was as though they had never been there.

And suddenly, seizing on one last, desperate hope, he turned to her. "Listen, this doesn't have to be goodbye, you know. We can write to each other—"

"Yes," she agreed immediately, and he saw the same spark of futile hope light her eyes. "I want to know everything that happens, all about your father and—"

"It's not as though neither of us knows how to dial a telephone. I can call you—"

"I'll write down my number." She moved to look for a piece of paper. "And you can give me your address and—"

Suddenly she stopped, and her shoulders sagged. Like a song without an ending, the desperate game they'd been playing faltered and died in midair. "We won't write to each other," she said softly.

She turned and looked at him, trying to smile. "We wouldn't know what to say. We'll be—different people, out there."

He nodded slowly. "I don't want to give you my phone number. I can't spend the rest of my life jumping every time the phone rings because it will never be you, will it?"

They looked at each other in helplessness and despair, aching for something to say, something they could do or promise or believe in, that would make everything different. But nothing came.

"Pam!"

The voice came from outside, but she didn't even turn her head toward it. Her heart was swelling, pounding, begging her not to do this thing. She whispered, "Alan..."

"Pam! Baby, are you there?"

It was Alan who moved his eyes toward the door. "We'd better go," he said.

Pam turned and walked outside.

Her father was trudging up the hill toward her, followed a few paces behind by two deputies. When he saw her he quickened his pace, and Pam ran the last few steps through the snow to him, letting him swing her off her feet in a fierce, fatherly embrace. She told herself that the tears that stung her eyes and clogged her throat were only relief and joy at being in her father's arms again. But she knew that wasn't so.

"Oh, sweetie, thank God you're all right!" He took her face in his hands and examined her closely. "Peter called us yesterday from New York and we've been combing the country for you ever since. We just found your car this morning.... Honey, you *are* okay? Your mother's been worried sick."

She made her smile as genuine as possible. "Of course I'm okay. I'm sorry I worried you, but..."

He dismissed that with a gesture and then his face sobered. "Honey, I'm so sorry about Peter. It must have been a terrible blow to you, and then being stranded in the storm on top of it..."

"It's okay, really. Everything's fine now. Daddy..." She turned and saw Alan approaching, slowly, still several steps away. She had to swallow hard before she could make her voice sound normal again. "Daddy, this is Alan Donovan. It was his car I almost hit."

Pam's father, whose faith in his daughter and the goodness of human nature would not allow him to do anything else, removed his glove and extended his hand to Alan warmly. "Well, young man, I'm glad to know my girl wasn't up here all by herself. Not that she couldn't take care of herself, but it's good to know there was a man here, just in case."

Alan shook his hand, and glanced at Pamela. "We kind of took care of each other, sir."

One of the deputies spoke up. "Well if that was your car down there, I reckon you'll be needing a ride to town. Looked to me to be in pretty bad shape."

Alan said, "I'd appreciate that."

"I can take him in the chopper," the deputy said, glancing at Pam's father. "I guess you'll be wanting to get your daughter back home."

Her father slipped a firm arm around Pam's shoulders. "I've got the Jeep down at the road. Come on, baby, let's not keep your mother waiting."

A stab of desperation struck Pam and she cast about for some way to stave it off. It couldn't be ending so quickly, so abruptly, in this frenzy of activity with all these people around . . . he couldn't disappear out of her life just like that.

She said quickly, "Daddy, I left the key in the cabin. Will you lock up for me?"

Her father glanced at her, and then at Alan, and there might have been a hint of puzzlement in his eyes. But he said, "Sure thing, sweetie. And come spring, remind me to deliver a whole cord of firewood to McMurty, free of charge."

She smiled vaguely at him, and then he started off toward the cabin. The two deputies struck up a conversation between themselves, and she and Alan were left alone.

She looked at him, and her throat was aching with all the things she wanted to say, her eyes hurt with the effort to imprint the memory of him, just as he was now, on her brain forever. Tall and lean, his silver hair glistening in the sun, his eyes quiet and clear and filled with her...Alan, whom she had loved forever, and would continue to love with all her heart for the rest of her life.

She heard the sound of the cabin door closing, and her father was returning. She said hoarsely, "Well. Take care of yourself."

He nodded. "You, too."

But there was more. So much more. And she couldn't begin to tell him even a part of it. He started to turn away, but she reached out her hand, and touched his fingers lightly.

"Alan...thank you. For making me feel special..." She tried to smile. "Even if it was only for a little while."

His fingers closed around hers. The sadness in his eyes was vast and deep, and it seemed to swallow up her heart. "I'm leaving the best part of myself here," he said, and brought their entwined fingers to her chest, over her heart. "With you."

"Ready to go," her father announced behind them.

Alan released her fingers, and smiled. He turned to join the deputy, and he did not look back as the two of them walked away.

Ten

___

February 12

Supper time in the Mercer household had always been the best time of day for Pam. There the family gathered to share their day: advice was dispensed, stories told and problems solved over a succulent home-cooked meal. But something had changed in the days since Pam had been home. The conversation was just as lively, her family's presence just as warm, her mother's pot roast just as inviting, but Pam couldn't seem to focus on any of it. Everything in her life was like that lately: diffused, out of touch and distant, as though she were walking through a cloud.

"Are you on another one of your diets?" her sister Kate demanded. Kate was a little plump and always took the efforts of other women to watch their figures as a personal insult.

"Who, me?" Pam looked down at her plate and realized that, although she had cut her meat into a dozen neat pieces, she hadn't eaten any of them. "No, I'm just not very hungry." She glanced apologetically at her mother. "I guess I must have overdosed on cookies at school."

But her mother knew her too well for that. She reached across the table and closed her hand on Pam's gently. "Honey, I know you won't believe me, but you will get over Peter. The hurt will go away. It just takes time, that's all. Meanwhile..." She gave Pam's fingers a reassuring squeeze. "Starving yourself is not going to make it any easier. Try to eat."

Pam forced a smile, but could not quite meet her mother's eyes. No one guessed that Peter had not crossed her mind once since she'd been home, and that sometimes, in fact, she almost didn't recognize his name when it was spoken. It was easier to let her family think her grief was caused by the man she had been engaged to for two years, rather than by a man she had known for less than three days.

Her father spoke into the awkward silence that fell, his voice sounding a little too loud as it always did when he was concerned about one of his fledglings and didn't know what to do to make it better. "By the way, Pam, I meant to tell you—guess who I saw today?"

She looked up without much interest. "Who, Daddy?"

"That young fellow's father—what's his name? Donovan."

Pam's heart skipped a beat and she almost dropped her fork. "Alan's father? He was here?"

Her father nodded, pleased to have distracted her. "He came to see about the car. Apparently his son told Phil down at the gas station to contact his father when it was ready. And you know what?" He frowned a little. "He didn't even want the car. Paid Phil for the repairs and told him to sell it, if he could. Can you believe that? A brand new-Porsche, and the man doesn't even want to take it home. They must have money."

Pam could hardly swallow. "Yes. They do."

Her father shrugged and reached for more potatoes. "Anyway, he seemed like a nice enough guy. Real worried about his son, though. Seems the first he'd heard about the accident was when Phil called about the car and he flew right out. He wanted to know if I knew where the boy went. You don't know, do you honey?"

Pam resisted the urge to massage her throat, it was so tight and aching. "I—uh, no. He said—I think he goes to school in Cambridge. I guess that's where he went."

"Odd behavior if you ask me, families that don't keep up with each other." Her father's tone had a disgruntled note to it. "I told him I'd start an investigation if he wanted, but the boy is over twenty-one."

"I'm sure . . . I'm sure it was just a matter of missed connections."

Her father nodded. "That's what he said. He's probably located him by now."

"Imagine," her mother murmured, buttering a roll. "Now where does Phil think he's going to find anyone around here who can afford to buy a Porsche?"

"I could sure use a new car, Daddy," Kate piped up, her eyes gleaming.

Her father guffawed. "In your dreams."

The voices went on around her as though waves were surging and receding from shore, but Pam didn't hear the words. There was a knot in her chest that felt as if a fist were squeezing the life out of her heart, and she was afraid if she took a deep breath she would burst into sobs.

It shouldn't be like this. What they had done was right; it was the only choice they had. They had separate lives, separate destinies, and they had known from the beginning that they must inevitably be apart. But, God, she had never expected it to hurt this much. She had never known how wide and deep the emptiness would be when he was gone, how pointless her days would seem without him in them, how long and dark the nights. She had been with him such a short time; how long could the pain possibly last?

Time, her mother had said. It would take time. Pam was sure she was right.

But she was very much afraid it would take a lifetime to get over the absence of Alan.

* * *

February 13

Alan lay on his bed, fully clothed, staring up at the ceiling. The day was gray and cold outside and a light snow fell. He did not think he would ever see snow again without thinking of Pam.

After accepting the deputy's ride into town, Alan had sold his Rolex for enough money for a bus ticket to Cambridge. It wasn't home, and it wasn't really where he wanted to be, but he hadn't been able to think of any place else to go. Once there he had spent a few days taking care of things, staying busy, refusing to think. He sold his television, VCR and stereo, and pawned some jewelry, but he didn't even know what he was going to do with all the cash. Getting rid of things simply made him feel a little better.

One night he had gone out with a bunch of guys he barely knew and had gotten blindly, stupidly drunk. It didn't blot Pam from his mind, and it didn't make the ache inside his chest go away. It merely made him sick.

He didn't contact his professors, and he didn't open a book. Most of the time he spent staring at the ceiling and doing nothing. That was easy. What he had to learn to do now was how to *feel* nothing.

There was a knock on the door, and he thought about ignoring it. But then some wild, irrational thought crossed his mind that one day he might open the door and it would be Pam. The same thing had happened with the phone; even though he knew she didn't have his number and would never call, every time the phone rang he had held his breath until he heard the voice on the other end. Finally he had unplugged it.

He got up and opened the door. His father stood there, immaculately tailored in a cashmere coat and calfskin gloves, his hat slightly splotched with melting snow, his handsome jaw clenched squarely. His eyes went over Alan once, briefly and assessingly, and he said, "Why don't you answer your damn phone?"

Alan stepped aside without replying, and his father strode in, tossing his hat on a chair and giving the apartment the same curt appraisal he had given his son before turning again. "Well," he demanded harshly, "don't you have anything to say for yourself?"

Alan said tiredly, "What are you doing here, Dad?"

It was amazing, how little he felt upon seeing his father. Not surprise, not anger, not even disappointment because it hadn't been Pam. It was as though the great black pit of his emotions swallowed up everything and dissolved it into a single neutral blur.

"What do you think? You take off from my place like a bat out of hell, the next thing I hear is from some Podunk town in Colorado about your wrecked car, I spend the next five days looking for your body..."

Then Alan was surprised. "It's not like I've never been in an accident before, Dad."

"This was different," Richard Donovan said gruffly.

Alan looked at his father carefully, faintly stirred by the realization that something odd was going on. His father had never come to see him before, not at any time, not in any place in the world. Alan was not even certain his father had ever even known where he was at any given time. Now, all of a sudden he was here, angry and upset. Why?

"Why did you come here?" Alan asked curiously. "You could have sent one of your flunkies, or hired a detective if you had trouble finding me. Why did you come yourself?"

"Because I was worried, damn it! Why else do you think I reported the car stolen? I wanted somebody to stop you, and make sure you were okay. That's all I ever wanted."

It took a moment for Alan to comprehend what the other man was saying, and when he did it was with a dull sort of wonder he could not fully accept. His father *cared* about him. He cared what became of him, he worried when he was gone. Why had Alan never realized that before? Why had his father never told him?

Richard Donovan ran a hand through his thick, gray hair and sucked in a tense breath. "It was a hell of a fight we had, son," he said after a moment. Alan could see the struggle in the older man's eyes, and he knew this was difficult for him. "I guess what I really wanted to say was—I'm sorry. And maybe the thing I'm sorriest for is that it took a thing like this—being scared within an inch of my life by that phone call from Colorado—to make me tell you so."

And just like that, in less than a moment and with only a few words, the pattern of a lifetime was changed. There should have been fanfare, drumrolls, flashing lights, but it was really very simple.

"I'm sorry too, Dad," Alan said, and that was all it took. The two men's eyes met and locked in understanding, and nothing else needed to be said. Things were not perfect between them and perhaps they never would be; all the problems weren't solved and there were many years of distance and misunderstanding between them yet to be bridged. But this was a beginning.

Richard Donovan cleared his throat and reached for his wallet. "Well, I guess you'll be needing some cash. I took care of that business with the Nevada police; I never meant for you to get in any trouble. I've had a new account set up for you at the bank and—"

Alan said, "Thanks, Dad." He looked at the bills in his father's hand and no one could have been more surprised than he was to hear himself saying, "But no thanks."

There was a startled flash in the other man's eyes, and perhaps just a trace of hurt. "What are you talking about? Look, I thought that other business was all behind us. Let's just wipe it off the board and start over."

"That's just what I want to do. And this time, I'd like to try and go it on my own."

"How?" his father demanded incredulously. "You've got to have money, you've got to live. What do you plan to do?"

Alan smiled. "Oh, I don't know. I might just get a job."

Richard Donovan stared at his son for a long time. At last he said, quietly, "You're serious about this, aren't you?"

Alan nodded.

His father slowly put the bills back into his wallet. When he looked at Alan again it was with a new kind of thoughtfulness, and even a measure of cautious respect. "You know, all these years—all I ever wanted was for you to grow up and take responsibility for yourself. Not that I wouldn't have liked to have you follow in the old man's footsteps, but I'm not too disappointed about that, as long as you know what you want."

"I do," Alan said. "Now." And he was amazed by the simplicity of it all. All he had ever needed was to know what he wanted, and he had found that in a mountain cabin in Colorado. It had simply taken him this long to realize it.

His father smiled at him. "Well, if you ever need a job..."

Alan smiled back. "Don't count on it, Dad. California is a little too far away from where I want to be."

There were questions in Richard Donovan's eyes, but he would not press. He turned toward the door, and then looked back. "Keep in touch, will you?"

"Right. I will."

The door was open, and his father was almost gone when Alan moved impulsively.

"Hey, Dad, I was thinking..."

His father turned back.

"If you don't have to catch a plane or anything...maybe we could go out and have a few beers together or something."

Richard Donovan smiled. "I can't think of anything I'd rather do," and the two of them left the building together.

February 14

The children had gone for the day, and the brightly painted walls of the school seemed to echo with silence. Pam sat at a low play table, picking through a heart-shaped box of candy one of the children had brought her, in no hurry to go home. She found herself staying late at school more and more these days, planning lessons, preparing bulletin boards and art projects or, more often than not, just sitting as she was today, doing nothing. Except that she wasn't really doing nothing. She was thinking about Alan.

She had thought—indeed, all logic dictated—that he would have faded from the forefront of her mind by now. In fact, he consumed more of her attention than ever, and grew larger and more vivid in her mind with each passing day. It was as though nothing real or important had happened to her since that weekend in the cabin; everything that had followed was merely a pale imitation of life. It made no sense, at all, but it was unmistakably true.

Terri, who was in charge of the three-year-old class, poked her head inside the door. "Oh, you're still here. I was getting ready to turn off the lights."

Pam glanced up. "Go ahead. I'll lock up."

Terri came inside, grimacing at the box of candy before Pam. "I got three of those things today. What is it about the mothers of three-year-olds that they think all teachers should be fat?"

"Well I think my mothers are beginning to catch on. None of them would take responsibility for this one. It was just sitting on my desk this morning and nobody remembered who brought it in."

Terri sat down across from Pam and helped herself to a butter cream. "Funny how much better a valentine tastes when it's from a lover." And then she paused, stricken by her own words. "Gosh, that was tactless of me. I'm sorry."

It took Pam a moment to realize Terri was referring to her breakup with Peter. Then she smiled. "Terri, let me ask you a hypothetical Valentine's Day question."

"Shoot."

Pam kept her eyes lowered, toying with the crinkly brown candy wrappers that littered the box. "Suppose you met this guy, a perfect stranger, completely by accident. Suppose you had absolutely nothing in common—different cultures, different backgrounds, different values, everything. Suppose he was completely irresponsible, never worked a day in his life, and suppose you'd only known him for a matter of days.... But suppose he understood you better than anyone you've ever known, he could practically read your mind and make you see things about yourself you never even guessed at before. And when you were with him you felt—I don't know, alive, and *validated* for the very first time. And suppose he loved you so much you could feel it in the air, and you loved him more than life itself . . . what would you do?"

Terri paused with a piece of candy halfway to her mouth, her eyes widening. "There's a choice?"

And then, pulling a straight face, she said, "Okay, hypothetical question." She chewed on the candy for a minute, and then looked back at Pam, serious now. "Right out of high school I met this guy named Joey. God, did I love that kid. He was a rock musician, can you believe it? And you know me, I still think Johnny Cash is the hottest thing going. But this guy..." Her eyes softened, becoming almost misty. "He could make my heart sing."

She focused on Pam again. "He joined this band, and they were going to Canada. He wanted me to go with him and there was nothing else in the world I wanted to do. I was flinging things in a suitcase, getting ready to run away with this guy my parents would have locked me up for even seeing, and suddenly it hit me. I didn't know anybody in Canada. What if the band failed? How would we eat? I didn't have anything in common with those people in the band, what if I hated it, how would I get home?" She gave a small, self-deprecating shrug. "So I let him get away."

"And now he's earning a million a week on MTV, right?"

Terri's expression was solemn and thoughtful. "No. The last I heard he was in Chicago, working for some kind of electronics firm. He never married. And me...I married Hal the dentist and he's given me three great kids and a house with only twenty years to go on the mortgage and a new car every five years. But he never, ever, made my heart sing," she finished softly.

She smiled at Pam, and there was wistfulness in her eyes. "So about this hypothetical fellow of yours, I wouldn't let him get away. I swear to God, Pam, if I had it all to do over again, I wouldn't let him get away."

Pam thought about Peter, whom she had never loved, and Alan, who made her heart sing. One had been a mistake, and the other...was too good to be true. And wasn't that what she had always been afraid of? That what she felt for Alan was only in her imagination, another mistake waiting to happen?

But it wasn't, she realized slowly. There was no comparison between Peter and Alan. What had happened in that snow-locked cabin hadn't been a mistake. Only fear had made her think that it was.

Pam reached across the table and squeezed her friend's fingers, trying to smile. But inside the tears were stinging and aching, because the truth was a painful thing. The only mistake she had made was in letting Alan go. And she was very much afraid that understanding had come too late.

March 23

Pam's mother closed the door on a gust of icy wind and turned back into the foyer, holding a florist's bouquet. "Pam!" she called. "For you!"

Pam came around the corner and her heart skipped when she saw the small vase of carnations and daisies her mother held. "Another one," her mother said, trying to keep the curiosity out of her tone. "One florist delivery every two weeks, just like clockwork. That truck has practically worn a rut in the driveway.''

Pam took the flowers, burying her face in them to hide the rush of color to her cheeks.

"No card, I suppose."

Pam made a cursory search, but wasn't surprised at what she found. There was never a card. But then, she didn't need one.

At first she had been genuinely perplexed by what her father referred to as her "secret admirer," then cautiously excited, and finally hardly able to believe what her heart dared to tell her. He hadn't forgotten her. It hadn't been just a dream. It was Alan.

Oh, how foolish she had been to imagine that what they had shared would fade with time. What absurd, unsubstantiated stumbling blocks she had put in their path with all her protestations about their love not standing the tests of the real world. *This* was the real world; hours spent thinking of him, nights passed aching for him, running to answer the phone hoping it might be him, searching the mail for a letter from him, listening for the sound of the florist's truck...living her life for him even when he wasn't here. Could anything be more real than what she was feeling now?

Pam's mother said gently, "Honey, I know you don't want to tell us who he is and the reasons why don't matter. I just want you to know I'm happy for you, and whoever he is, I approve."

Pam looked at her mother in surprise. "But—you don't even know him."

Her mother smiled and patted her cheek. "I know all I need to know. He's put a glow in your eyes and color in your cheeks, and you're in love with him. That's all that matters, isn't it?"

Pam buried her face in the flowers again and let the sweet, intoxicating fragrance sweep through her like a benediction. *Yes*, she thought. *That's all that matters.*

April 3

Pam slammed down the telephone and could have cried with frustration. After over a month of working up her courage, three days of telephone calls to and from Cambridge, Massachusetts, she had discovered...nothing. The Alan Donovan the university had listed as an alumnus was no longer actively enrolled, but they were able to supply her with the last known telephone number. The telephone had been disconnected.

At her elbow was the latest florist delivery, a living arrangement of yellow and red tulips. They reminded her of the tulips Alan had described for her in her London dream, and when she looked at them she had to blink back a sting of tears. Almost three months now, flowers, candy, never a card, never a note. Every day she told herself, *Today will be the day he'll call, or I'll get a letter... a postcard, a telegram, something.* But every day passed and there was nothing.

He's afraid, she finally decided. *He thinks I may not want to hear from him, that I've forgotten him, that I don't love him any more. He's waiting for a sign from me.*

That was when she decided, though it was the hardest thing she had ever done in her life, to contact him. And she'd failed.

Anger warred with despair and she didn't know what to do. How did he expect her to get in touch with him if she didn't know where he was? How could she tell him she loved him if his telephone was disconnected? How could she tell him how sorry she was, what a horrible, foolish mistake she'd made, if she didn't even know his last address? How could he do this to her?

The anger faded and despair took over. Maybe the flowers weren't from him. Maybe it was all just some pervert's idea of a joke or, more likely, some well-meaning family member trying to cheer her up and she had imagined the whole thing. Maybe Alan was in Acapulco or South America and he had completely forgotten about her. Maybe she had been right all along: it was impossible between them. They simply weren't meant to be together.

But she didn't believe that. Not for a minute. She bowed her head into her folded arms on her desk and tried not to cry. *Why didn't he call?*

May 1

"Anything for me, Mom?"

Pam did not know why she bothered to ask. A sensible woman would have given up hope months ago.

But there had been no flowers this week and hope, sensible or not, was all she had left.

Pam's mother sorted through the mail and handed Pam a card. "Just another notice from the library, dear. Are you sure you don't have materials over-due?"

Pam stared at the card in her hand, and the bitterness was so thick in her throat that for a moment she couldn't speak. "I'm sure, Mom."

"Well, I just can't imagine why they keep sending you those notices. Six in the past two weeks, a waste of taxpayers' money if you ask me. If I were you I'd go right down there and get it straightened out."

Pam looked at the card without seeing it for a moment longer, then abruptly she stuffed it into her pocket. "That's just what I'm going to do," she declared, and stalked out of the house. Today she needed to yell at somebody, and if the only person available was old Mrs. Perkins down at the library, so be it. If she didn't do something, anything, soon, she would go out of her mind.

The glory of springtime in the Rockies which she once had loved so much was lost on Pam as she got into her car and drove the three miles to town. Pasture land was beginning to green, calves were sunning themselves and foals were playing chase in the balmy clear air, wildflowers were peeking through the mud on the sides of the road. The world was renewing itself, proudly emerging from the strife of the winter bigger and brighter than ever. But Pamela Mercer had left her heart in a snowbound cabin on the mountain, and spring was not a welcome sight to her.

What had become of him? Had he finally given up on her? Had something happened to him, was he sick or hurt or lost somewhere, unable to take care of himself? Was that why the flowers had stopped? Or had he simply gotten tired of waiting for her, and taken her silence as refusal?

But what was she supposed to *do*? She had racked her brain, formulating and rejecting one outrageous plan after another, in an effort to find a way to locate him. But there must be something....

His father. It occurred to Pam so suddenly, and with such absolute certainty, that she slammed on the brakes outside the library, causing her tires to squeal. She could call *his father*. He was an important man, the head of a company, he shouldn't be too hard to find. He might not know where Alan was, but he could find out. A year ago, even six months ago, the prospect of contacting such an important, powerful man as Richard Donovan, a man she didn't even know, would have intimidated her beyond all imagining. She could never have brought herself to do such a thing. But now all she could think of was how stupid she was not to have done it before. Of course. All she had to do was find out how to locate him, and what better place to start than the public library?

Her mind was racing with excitement, and she had almost forgotten her original purpose for coming here. At the last minute, she pulled out the crumpled notice from her pocket, striding through the door. "Mrs. Perkins, I wanted to talk to you about—"

The words froze in her throat. The person who looked up from the desk wasn't Mrs. Perkins. It was a light-haired young man in a gray cable-knit sweater and wire-rimmed glasses. With a smile that melted her heart.

"May I help you?"

Pam took two uncertain steps toward the desk. She had some vague faraway notion that she might be hallucinating. Her voice was hoarse and sounded as though it belonged to someone else. "I came to see— about this." She held out the notice at arm's length.

Alan reached across the desk and took it from her, smiling. "I see you got my message."

Alan. It was Alan, and it didn't matter what he was doing here or how he had gotten here or whether she was dreaming it all; it was *Alan*. Her heart twisted and leaped into a spiraling, shrilling rhythm and she wanted to shout, she wanted to cry. And all she could do was look at him. She could have looked at him forever.

At last she came closer to the desk. She could smell his cologne. She wondered if a person could die from joy. She wondered if she dared believe what was happening to her. And all she could think of to say was, softly, "I like your glasses. They make you look like a young Robert Redford."

He inclined his head modestly and touched the rims. "Thanks. I think so, too." But behind the glasses his clear gray eyes were hungry, searching her face, drinking her in, leaping and questioning and speaking without words.

Someone came to the desk with a stack of books. Alan ignored him. "Guess what I've got?" Alan said.

Me, Pam thought. *Me, forever...*

"A job," he told her, when she couldn't speak.

With difficulty, she dragged her eyes away from him to take in their surroundings, briefly. "So I see."

"This?" He gave a deprecating shrug. "This is just to keep you in candy and flowers. I mean a real job. Starting fall quarter, I'm the new English teacher at Raintree County High."

It was too much. Too much and too grand, and she could not take it in. All she wanted to do was hold him, to press her face against the soft texture of his sweater and wrap her arms around his waist and feel his muscles, hear his heartbeat, listen to his breathing...

"All this time..." Her throat caught unexpectedly on a breath with a little choking sound. "The flowers and—the valentine—it was from you, wasn't it? But you never called, you never..."

"I felt you needed a proper courtship," he said.

"I could kill you." But her words lost some of their ferocity because she couldn't stop smiling. She thought her face would break with the width of her smile.

"And," he admitted, sobering somewhat, "I didn't want to push you. I guess I was a little afraid that I might push you away. You said time would tell and, the fact is, about all I've had to give you these past few months is time."

"Excuse me..." The man with the books was becoming impatient.

"I tried to reach you," Pam said quickly, as though afraid he might disappear if she delayed too long. Even the man who was waiting to check out books represented a chance she couldn't afford to take. "I've been going crazy trying to figure out how to reach you. I called the university, and I was going to call your father—"

"I only got here two weeks ago," Alan said softly, and with the same kind of rapid intensity to his voice that was in hers. "I was so worried I couldn't work things out with the job and everything, and since I've been here it's been hell, trying to work up the nerve to call you, wondering how you'd react, hoping every day you'd come in here. You really should read more, you know that?"

Pamela reached across the desk and his hands found hers immediately. The warmth of his grip went through her like a potent intoxicant and it was all she could do to keep from laughing out loud with joy. "I'll keep that in mind."

"Is there anybody here who works for the library?" the man at the desk said loudly.

Alan didn't turn around. His eyes were locked on hers and he couldn't seem to stop smiling, either. "I'm going to lose my job."

"You always were irresponsible."

There was a deepening, and a softening in his eyes. "I'm a different person now, Pam."

"So am I," she answered softly, "because of you. But one thing hasn't changed. I still love you more than I ever thought it was possible for anyone to love."

She saw his gentle inhalation of breath, and his fingers tightened on hers. "So. It's going on four months now. Do you think that's long enough?"

"For what?"

"For us to know each other." His eyes held hers, steady and tender and full of things she could spend a lifetime examining and understanding, and treasuring. "Before we get married."

"I think," Pam whispered, "it's more than enough."

The man at the desk left his books and stalked out.

Neither Pam nor Alan noticed. Pam leaned over the desk, and curved her hand around Alan's shoulder. Alan's fingers cupped her neck and their lips met in a long and glorious kiss. And that was only the beginning.

*   *   *   *   *

SILHOUETTE Desire

COMING NEXT MONTH

#535 WILDERNESS CHILD—Ann Major
December's *Man of the Month*, Tad Jackson, wasn't about to be burned twice by the woman who'd betrayed him—but the fire between him and Jessica Bancroft Kent raged out of control.

#536 THE DIAMOND'S SPARKLE—Celeste Hamilton
Public relations man Nathan Hollister lived his life the same way he drove his car...fast. Beautiful Liz Patterson could be the one obstacle that slowed him down!

#537 HALFWAY TO HEAVEN—Katherine Granger
Lindsey Andrews wanted it all—the perfect career *and* the perfect man. Jed Wentworth offered her both, but she couldn't mix business with pleasure—could she?

#538 BEDSIDE MANNER—Jo Ann Algermissen
Though her job was at stake, Dr. Kristie Fairbanks was tempted to give in to Joshua Hayden, the one man who could threaten her career...and her heart.

#539 READ BETWEEN THE LINES—Erica Spindler
Sociology professor Katherine Reed needed a roommate for a research experiment, and her old "friend" Michael Tardo kindly volunteered. Unfortunately, he was still charming...and she was still in love.

#540 CHRISTMAS STRANGER—Joan Hohl
It was a cold, snowy night when Virginia Greyson met Matthew Hawk. He was the gift of a lifetime. But would fate take him as it had so mysteriously brought him?

AVAILABLE NOW:

#529 SHILOH'S PROMISE
BJ James

#530 INTERLUDE
Donna Carlisle

#531 ULTERIOR MOTIVES
Laura Leone

#532 BLUE CHIP BRIDE
Audra Adams

#533 SEEING IS BELIEVING
Janet Bieber

#534 TAGGED
Lass Small

SILHOUETTE DESIRE™
presents
AUNT EUGENIA'S TREASURES
by CELESTE HAMILTON

Liz, Cassandra and Maggie are the honored recipients of Aunt Eugenia's heirloom jewels...but Eugenia knows the real prizes are the young women themselves. Every other month from December to April in Silhouette Desire, read about Aunt Eugenia's quest to find them worthy men and a treasure more valuable than diamonds, rubies or pearls—lasting love.

Coming in December: THE DIAMOND'S SPARKLE

Altruistic attorney Liz Patterson balks at Aunt Eugenia's attempt at matchmaking. Clearly, a shrewd PR man isn't her type. Nathan Hollister, after all, likes fast cars and fast times, but, as he tells Liz, love is something he's willing to take *very* slowly.

In February: RUBY FIRE

Passionate Cassandra Martin has always been driven by impulse. After traveling from city to city, seeking new opportunities, Cassandra returns home...ready to re-kindle the flame of young love with the man she never forgot, Daniel O'Grady.

In April: THE HIDDEN PEARL

Maggie O'Grady loved and lost early in life. Since then caution has been her guide. But when brazen Jonah Pendleton moves into the apartment next door, gentle Maggie comes out of her shell and glows in the precious warmth of love.

Aunt Eugenia's Treasures
Each book shines on its own, but together
they're priceless

SD-AET-1